RUNAWAY
BY SABINE WILDER

CHAPTER 1
DOGS AND ROSES

Susan Wolfe drove along the crumbling back road with the car windows rolled down, letting the smell of autumn rush over her. It was warm for October and she wanted to enjoy the nice weather while it lasted. The wind whipped her long hair into a golden froth covering her face. Pushing the tangle back from her eyes, she took a deep breath of the rich air. It was going to be a beautiful day, unfortunately she would be caged inside a classroom for the rest of it.

The Honda Civic jolted over a bump in the road, eliciting a curse from Susan. One of the detriments of Canadian winters was what they did to the roads. The small town of Timber Creek, nestled in the wilderness of Northern Ontario, was no exception. The road smoothed out as Susan entered a suburb. Trees gave way to houses and lawns, while the scent of autumn leaves diminished, replaced by lawn clippings.

Susan pulled over in front of a two storey house with grey siding. The trees in the yard cast their long morning shadows on the curb, but they didn't reach the car as Susan pulled to the side of the road and parked it.

No sooner had the Civic rolled to a stop than the door of the house flew open and a girl ran down the driveway. The passenger side door wrenched open and she scrambled inside, "You're late!"

"Relax Anna! On a day like this, no one will even be inside by the time we get there. We're not going to be late." Susan said.

Anna buckled herself in before brushing at stray locks of her short hair. Susan wanted to tell her she looked fine, but knew better than to interrupt Anna's fussing. For a brief moment, the sun caught the chestnut highlight to Anna's dark hair and eyes, before she shot Susan an irritated look, "Let's go!"

"We have plenty of time!" Susan pulled away from the curb. "Don't worry so much!"

Anna gave up on her hair and grinned at Susan. "Easy for you to say. If it wasn't for me, you'd be late every day from stopping to smell the flowers Miss Wolfe."

"Don't go there." Susan laughed, but it rang hollow failing to hide her unease.

"Fine." Anna let the matter drop. "So what's new with you?"

"Our cross-country running meet is this weekend! I can't wait!" The thought of competition electrified Susan.

"Ugh, great. You're going to be hyper all week."

"Nah, I'll be fine!" As hard as it was going to be to spend all week trapped in a classroom, the anticipation of the open trails made it bearable. "You should join the club! Sports teams look great on university applications."

"How many times have we had this conversation? I suck at everything athletic and I definitely can't run. Besides, I don't think it's going to matter so much now that we're in our last year of high school."

"It would still be fun! You should give sports a chance. What have you got to lose?"

"Oh sure," Anna's voice dripped sarcasm, "Why don't I try out for the basketball team this season! I'll just run between everyone's legs."

"Aw come on... you're not *that* short."

"I think the lack of oxygen in the air up there is messing with your brain. Besides," Anna grew quiet as she gazed out the window, "Even if I was magically struck with some kind of athletic ability, I doubt your teammates would be excited."

"They're not all bad you know." Susan cringed. She was treading dangerous water. While she managed to navigate through social storms with ease, Anna wasn't always so lucky. Susan never understood why. Despite her shyness and anxiety, Anna was a great person.

"It doesn't matter. I'll always be a loser in their eyes."

Her best friend's resignation only made Susan want to fight harder. "That's why you should join the cross-country club and prove them wrong!"

"You don't know when to give up do you?" Anna's expression softened. "As much as I appreciate your undying faith in my non-existent athletic ability, I think I'll stick to my geekier pursuits." Anna grew thoughtful, "Maybe you should take up one of my hobbies. The dark room is pretty cozy you know."

"With all those chemicals you need to develop film, I'm sure I'd find a way to blow everything up."

"It would be fun! You should give photography a chance!"

Trust Anna to throw Susan's own argument back at her. Stumped for a comeback, Susan was now wary that whatever she said might be used against her later.

Anna dropped the sarcasm, "Would it make you happy if I came out to your meet this weekend to cheer you on?"

"Really? Are you sure you won't get bored sitting around waiting for me to cross the finish line?"

"I think it'll be nice to spend some time outside. Maybe I'll take my camera and take some photos before all the leaves are gone..." Anna trailed off, losing herself in thought. "Yeah, that sounds like a good plan."

That was all Susan needed. Once Anna committed to a plan, she was going through with it. "Great! Don't forget to save some film for a pic of me on the podium!"

"If you make it that far."

"Challenge accepted!" Susan didn't try to tone down her excitement. This weekend would be amazing.

The Honda pulled into a decrepit parking lot behind Timber Creek Secondary School. As Susan stepped out of the car, the smell of damp bricks drying in the sun hit her nostrils. Then the more noxious fumes of the parking lot invaded her senses. Oil and grease from old vehicles hung heavy in the air mixing with cigarette smoke.

The first bell rang and Anna tugged on Susan's sleeve. "Come on! Hurry up!"

Susan shouldered her backpack, following Anna to the door. One last breath of sweet autumn air filled her lungs before the door clanged shut behind them.

Being stuck indoors all day used to drive Susan crazy. To some extent it still did. She had a very sensitive sense of smell and being stuck inside a box reeking of cleaning chemicals and the body odor of twenty other kids was agonizing. It was an assault on her senses compared to the fresh air of the outdoors or the comforting smells of her home. It didn't help that no one understood her discomfort. Susan fought many long battles with her mother, trying to explain why she hated being stuck in school all day. Eventually she stopped trying to explain. No one understood what she was talking about. No one except Anna.

Susan remembered the day she told her best friend about her biggest insecurity. Back when they were kids, sitting outside on Susan's front porch, soaking up the warmth of a spring day. Rain had made the ground swell with the hearty scent of earth. Green shoots pierced the soil and the first flowers were budding.

"What are you thinking about Sue?" Anna asked from her

seat on a padded lawn chair on the porch.

"Hmm, what?" Susan jerked her attention away from the smell of the natural world around her, embarrassed to be caught engrossed in it.

"It must be something good, you were really spaced out!" Anna giggled.

"I was not!" Susan snapped. She immediately regretted her tone, but she felt defensive.

Anna proceeded with caution. "You wanna talk about it?"

"What for?"

"Because you always want to talk!" Anna's doe-like eyes opened wide, "Is it a secret?"

"No... not really." It wasn't. Susan had told lots of people, but other kids thought she was weird and adults didn't get it at all. It wasn't that she couldn't talk about it, she just didn't want to.

"I promise I won't tell anyone."

Anna didn't have to say it. Susan knew her friend would take any secret she told her to the grave, but the promise reassured her none the less. Susan sought the right words to explain it one more time. "I was thinking about the way things smell after the rain."

"And?" Anna encouraged her to continue.

Susan shrugged, "That's it."

"That's it? That's what your worried about? Smelling the flowers?"

"Not just the flowers! Everything! I can smell the soil, the rain, the budding trees, the new grass, the dead leaves..." Susan trailed off when she saw Anna's blank expression staring back at her.

"That's... a lot of different things." Anna drew the words out slowly.

"Forget it! I knew you wouldn't understand." Susan was wasting her time trying to explain it.

"Well..." Anna looked out over the yard. "I can smell the

soil after the rain too. It's pretty. But all the other stuff you said, I've never noticed before. What's it like?"

A spark of hope lit inside Susan. "Are you serious or are you teasing like everyone else?"

"Are you serious? Are you pulling my leg to make me look dumb when the punchline comes?"

"No! I swear I'm not making this up!" Susan tried to sound as sincere as she could. She couldn't lose Anna now. "You don't know what it's like. I've tried explaining it so many times, but no one gets it!"

"Try me."

"OK," Susan had to resist the urge to bolt from the porch and run as far and fast as she could. "You know how some people are visual and think in images or whatever? Well, sometimes I think in smells."

Anna went silent. Susan gave her some time to let things sink in but Anna struggled to grasp the concept, "So, you see in smells? Like a dog or something?"

"I'm not a dog!"

"I know you're not a dog! I didn't mean it like that! I guess it's... I don't know what to say!" Anna threw her hands up in surrender.

Susan immediately regretted letting her frustration get the better of her. Anna was trying. "Sorry. I know it's hard to find the right words. Believe me, I've been trying to describe this since I was born, but it never comes out right."

"This really bothers you doesn't it?"

Susan's defenses flared, but she reigned them in. "You try explaining something to other people all your life and having no one get it! Some of them even make fun of you for it!"

Anna grew reflective, speaking more to herself than to Susan, "That's not as crazy as you might think it sounds."

"Well I feel like I'm going crazy!"

"It's OK Sue. I believe you and I'm pretty sure you're not crazy."

The tension in Susan's body drained away, and the urge to run away screaming faded. "I've always noticed smells that other people don't. I see the world around me through my nose, differently than everyone else. It's so weird and what's weirder is that nobody ever wants to talk about it! I feel like a freak."

"Just because something about you makes you different, doesn't mean you're a freak. If that's the case, we're all freaks!"

"Well, it's good to know I'm not alone."

Anna stuck her tongue out and Susan couldn't help but laugh. She had been taking herself too seriously. Gratefully, Anna brought things back into perspective.

"So tell me," Anna asked, "What do I smell like?"

Susan paused to think about it. "No one's ever asked me that before. I don't know if I have the words to describe it."

"Try!" Anna bounced on the edge of her seat, eager for an answer.

Susan took a deep breath. "It's like... if smells were colours, you'd be light, not white, but maybe a yellowy light. Bright, light, and warm. Like a Sunbeam! Does that sound dumb?"

"No way! This is fun! What else?"

"You smell kind of sweet too. With something green in there, like growing... no that's not right, not like a plant or anything... ugh, now I know I sound dumb!"

"You get all that from me!? No way!"

"It's true, I swear!" Susan summoned every ounce of sincerity she had. "Every person is different and complicated like that, and it's so hard to describe. I know it sounds messed up, but I'm not making anything up!"

"I believe you Sue, but it's..."

"Weird? Hard to believe? I know!" Susan rose from her seat and paced the short stretch of porch in front of her. "OK, my mom's making dinner, can you smell it?"

Anna shook her head, watching Susan as she paced back and forth.

Susan breathed in deeply, "Mashed potatoes, chicken and ugh... broccoli."

Anna rose to stand beside Susan, sniffing the air. "I don't smell anything."

The door to the house opened and Susan's mother called out to the girls. "Anna would you like to stay for supper?" The blast of air from inside the house carried with it the aroma of food.

"Smells good Mom, what's for dinner?"

"Oh just chicken and mashed potatoes." She checked with Anna again, "I hope you like broccoli!"

Anna was silent for a few seconds before her manners kicked in, "Uh, sure! I'd love to stay for dinner but I need to call my parents to let them know."

"Of course!" Susan's mother crooned. "It's nice to see some kids still think about their parents in this day and age."

Susan registered her mother's jab, but let it slide. Her attention was focused on Anna's reaction.

A timer chimed in the kitchen and Mrs. Wolfe retreated back inside. "Finish up whatever you're doing, dinner will be ready soon!"

The door shut leaving the two girls alone outside. Susan stared intently at Anna, who struggled to find her voice again.

"You were right," Anna gave Susan a suspicious sideways look. "Seriously, if you're doing this as a joke it's not funny!"

"You're right it's not funny. Of all the superpowers in the world, I get a keen sense of smell! Lamest superpower ever!"

"Don't worry, I'll still let you be my trusty sidekick."

Susan laughed in relief. She didn't understand it herself, but Anna was willing to accept whatever freaky abilities she had. It was nice to have someone to confide in.

CHAPTER 2
CHEMISTRY

The reek of the science lab roused Susan from her memories as she opened the door. Even someone with a poor sense of smell would notice the odors inside. Dusty textbooks from the 80's lined the shelves along with various glassware and curios. The tang of gas permeated the air, on top of the scent of chemicals and powdery chalk from the blackboard. It was enough to make Susan gag, but she trudged inside, forcing herself to sit in her seat. It wouldn't be so bad after everyone settled and the class started.

Susan sat at a bench in the middle of the lab, but the blue sky peeking through the windows distracted her. It was a crime to be stuck inside this torture chamber when it was so beautiful outside. Anna sat down next to her, taking out her notes with methodical care.

Susan slumped in her chair, suppressing the urge to run over and stick her head out the window. As she reached into her bag for her notes, her eye caught the empty bench behind her. At least there was one good thing about chemistry class. The bench behind them was occupied by two of the hottest guys in school.

One of the stools behind her scraped against the linoleum floor, grabbing Susan's attention. She greeted the tall, lean boy who drifted into his seat, "Morning Will. How's it going?"

The boy ran pale fingers through his dark locks – which were always somehow perfectly messy, "I'm fine, yourself?"

Susan's insides melted a little. William Murray was the dream boy of Timber Creek Secondary for a reason. He could melt any girl's heart with a smile. Will was more than a pretty face though, he had a way about him that put people at ease. He came to Timber Creek only last year. Apparently, his father moved around a lot and frequently left on business trips, leaving the Murray household open to whatever social events Will concocted. This cemented his good standing with the popular kids, but Will never let his status go to his head. He was always friendly to Susan and Anna.

The wind rattled the panes of the lab windows, beckoning Susan with the promise of fresh air. "I wish I was outside right now," she said honestly.

"Me too. It's so nice out today. But what can you do?" Will shrugged, resigning himself to their situation. Then his eyes softened as his attention shifted to the other girl in front of him. "Right Anna?"

Anna tensed. "Uh huh," she muttered without facing him.

Susan didn't understand Anna's behavior. She was often uncomfortable around others, but around Will, Anna became completely dysfunctional. Susan thought maybe Anna had a crush on him, but Anna fervently denied that was the case. Susan couldn't put her finger on it, but there was something between Anna and Will.

"Isn't it rude not to look at someone when they're talking to you?" Will asked Susan, loud enough for Anna to hear.

The dark haired girl spun around in her seat, confronting the boy behind her, "Isn't it rude to keep bothering someone when they've told you to leave them alone!"

"Easy guys!" Susan threw up her hands as if getting

between a fist fight. "Geez, class hasn't even started and you're at it like an old married couple!"

Anna's glare was so cold Susan swore the temperature in the room dropped. Anna went back to her notes concentrating on writing the date in the top corner of the page and ignoring everything else. Susan cringed. She had really stepped in it this time.

"I'm sorry Sue, you shouldn't be made to feel like a third wheel!" Will brushed off the encounter. "Of course if my lab partner ever showed up on time, that wouldn't be a problem now would it?"

Heat crept up Susan's cheeks and suddenly her mind went blank. A witty retort was right there on the tip of her tongue, but she couldn't get it out.

The door burst open and a tall, brawny boy with short dark hair stumbled into the classroom, his tan skin flushed from running to class. He scanned the lab for their teacher who had yet to arrive. "Yes! Beat Mr. N!"

"Barely." A deadpan voice from the hall made the boy jump as their teacher, Mr. Neal, ushered him inside. The bell for class rang, drowning out the laughter in the lab.

"Please take your seat Jim." Mr. Neal instructed.

Unfazed by the commotion his entrance had caused, Jim sauntered over to his seat beside Will. As he swung onto his stool he flashed Susan a smile. This time Susan really did feel her insides melt.

Jim Schenn was the captain of the senior boys hockey team; an athletic, handsome and popular guy. In short, he was out of Susan's league, but that never stopped her from dreaming. Jim had dated the same girl, for most of his high school career, but they had broken up at the end of the summer. The rumor was that Jim had cheated on her, but the rumor mill has its way of spinning out of control. Susan didn't know the real story and wasn't about to judge. Jim was still as popular as ever among the girls, perhaps even more so now that he was single. Susan had liked him since ninth grade, but never had the opportunity to talk to him. All that changed with this chemistry class.

Susan controlled her excitement, calming herself with deep breaths. Unfortunately, in the science lab this agitated a sneeze.

"Bless you!" Came a hiss from behind her.

Susan peered over her shoulder, catching Jim grinning at her. Dimples lit up his face and the rest of the room dimmed out of Susan's vision.

"Hey, um, you got a pen I could borrow?" Jim scratched at the back of his head. "I was kind of in a rush this morning."

"When are you not in a rush in the morning?" Susan kicked herself for letting her wit get the better of her, but Jim appeared unscathed, almost amused by her joke. As she passed him a pen, Jim gave her a wink, whispering, "Thanks! You're the best!" Despite being a bit of a clown, Jim had his charm.

The day droned on, class after class. By the final bell Susan wanted to tear all the doors off their hinges for standing between her and her cross-country running practice.

Susan jogged across the back parking lot and down a steep hill into the bowl of the football field. A gravel track ran its way around the field and a few students had congregated on a spot at the track's edge. Trees lined the far side of the field, leading down an even steeper hill into a gully. On the other side of the bowl, the school buildings blocked the view of the suburbs. Susan was in her own little world. A world where she was in charge.

The sun cast its golden afternoon light at a low angle drawing out long shadows. The light faded faster every day. A reminder that even with the warm weather, winter was around the corner. Susan soaked in the sun and the smell of leaves in the air, wishing autumn would stay a little longer. A chill crawled up her spine, despite the warmth of the sun, urging her to make the most of this moment.

Susan's teammates were stretching by the edge of the track as their coach, Ms. Nelson, fussed over her clipboard. Greetings went around and Susan prepared to start the warm-up when someone pointed up at the back parking lot. "Maybe we should wait for him."

Susan looked over her shoulder. Jim jogged down the dusty slope the way she had just come. When he caught her eye, he waved. Susan's chest tightened, but then a grin spread across her face in spite of trying to hold it back. "We'll get started," she said.

Susan led the warm-up making an effort not to pay attention to Jim as he greeted the coach. He talked to her forever until finally he ambled up to the team. "Hey guys, sorry I'm late!"

"Hey Jim," Susan waved him into the group. "Does this mean you're joining us?"

"Yeah, I thought it would be a good workout to get in shape for hockey season. Anyone can join right?"

"Yup, all you have to do is show up for practice," Susan glanced at Jim sideways through a stretch, "Preferably on time, if you think you can handle that."

A couple students giggled. Jim didn't seem to mind and threw Susan a mock salute, "Yes Ma'am!"

"OK!" Susan addressed her tiny group of runners, "We've got a meet coming up this weekend so the more practices you can make the better." Susan naturally fell into the role of captain of the team. Not because she was the most experienced or had the best records, but because her passion for running got everyone else excited. "Today we're going to work on endurance. It's about stamina over speed, so find a pace that works for you. Let's see how many laps we can do in five minutes at a steady pace! Coach Nelson will start us off and stop us with the whistle. Pay attention to your energy level. I want 75 to 80 percent, not 110. Save that for later!"

Susan took up a spot on the track at the back of the team. She wanted to keep an eye on their starts, even though she would most likely overtake them. Then they would be on their own. Her limbs trembled with anticipation and she bounced up and down on her toes trying to shake out the jitters. In that moment before running, even Jim's presence was a dim focus in her mind.

The whistle blew. Susan let everyone get a few paces ahead before taking off from the start at an easy run. Everyone looked good except for one person pulling way ahead of the group.

"Slow down Jim! Eighty percent max! Concentrate on your pace." Susan yelled.

Jim slowed a bit, but wouldn't surrender his place at the front of the pack. Susan held back her competitive streak. Not yet. She drew up behind Jim, letting him set the pace for the first few laps. It was easy going for Susan, but for anyone not used to distance running, keeping the pace Jim had set for more than a few minutes would be exhausting. Sweat poured down Jim's face but it was his breathing that gave him away. A few minutes in and Jim was struggling for air.

Susan stepped up her speed, pulling away from the group and leaving Jim in the dust. Susan loathed ditching her own drill, but it would be worth it for the lesson Jim would learn. Jim tried to keep up, but there was no way he could match Susan. This was her track, her sport. Susan was in charge here and no one could take that away from her. The track flew by under her feet, and every muscle flexed to her purpose. She didn't notice her crazy pace until she had come up behind Jim again.

"Thirty seconds!" Coach Nelson called out.

Time to give it everything she had. Susan sped past Jim who was struggling to keep even a slow pace. It was too easy. Susan let herself go and ran to her fullest, pushing herself to go faster. The whistle blew. Susan pushed the last few strides to finish her lap, before succumbing to the whistle.

She slowed to a walk, tilting her head back to look at the sky. It was too brilliant a blue to appreciate fully as the sun swam in her eyes. She gasped for breath, then focused on returning her breathing to normal.

"Good job guys!" Susan said between breaths. "Walk a couple laps to cool down, then we'll meet in the middle."

Susan walked over to a lump lying on the grass outside the track. She gave Jim's foot a little nudge with her toe. "Walk it off. It's better for you than stopping completely."

Jim sat up wiping the sweat from his face. "How do you do it?"

Susan swelled with smug pride, "Practice."

"I mean, I could do it too," Jim jumped to his feet, "I could sprint like that, but I'd be dying afterwards!"

"Well, it might help if you follow my advice instead of trying to beat everyone else."

"I was only doing eighty percent like you said!" Jim said unabashed.

"I don't think that means what you think it means. You need to drop it down further then. The point isn't going fast it's maintaining yourself over the long run."

"I guess I'm not used to that," Jim admitted, scratching his head self-consciously. "Maybe you could give me some pointers?"

"That's what we're here for."

"Yeah but uh... maybe you could help me out one on one. I've got a lot to figure out and everyone else seems to know what they're doing."

It was a good thing Susan's cheeks were already flaming from her run. She had to appreciate Jim's obviousness, but it couldn't hurt to play with him a bit more, "I don't know, you think you can listen?"

"Of course! I'm here to learn from you!"

"Good, 'cause practice ain't over! We've got a lot more work to do and I'll make sure you get some tailored advice."

CHAPTER 3
RACE

"Maybe you should take a jacket?" Susan's mother rummaged through the front closet looking for something to fuss over.

Susan grabbed her track bag, slinging it over her shoulder. "I have my hoodie, I'll be fine Mom."

"What about a hat?"

"Mom! It's like 20 degrees outside and I'll be running!"

"Sunglasses? You should be protecting your eyes."

Susan clenched and opened her fists slowly. The last thing she needed was a fight with her mother right before the meet. Instead of arguing, she reached for the door, "I gotta go Mom. Anna will be here any minute and I don't want to be late!"

"Good luck sweetie!" Susan's mom called out, but was cut off by the shutting door.

As Susan leaned her back into the closed door, a pang of guilt rippled through her stomach. Her mom meant well, but she had to dote on every little thing and it drove Susan crazy. At least these were minor spats over stupid things. Susan rarely saw eye to eye with her mother on anything, but she would take her mother's fussing over a real argument any day.

Susan took a deep breath and stepped out from the overhang of the porch into the sunshine. It was a gorgeous day. The breeze was slight, pushing clouds across a piercingly blue sky and rustling the leaves in the trees. The heat of summer was gone, but the biting cold of winter had yet to set in. The temperature was just right. It was the perfect day for running.

Susan sat on the porch steps, drinking in the lush scents around her. Her family lived just outside of suburbia, on the fringe of the bush. Trees surrounded the house on every side except where the driveway cut through them. White birches set the stage with their yellowing leaves, backed up by a host of green pine and spruce. Splashes of intense red or fiery orange came from the maples. The oaks had yet to turn. They were always the last to lose their leathery brown leaves, sometimes clinging to their branches even after the snow set in.

Trails cut swaths through the lawn from the house to the bush, where they continued to weave in and out of the Wolfe property. Susan knew those trails well. Whenever she fought with her mother, that was where she escaped, whether to blow off steam after an argument, or to avoid a fight altogether. Running down the trails became a regular exercise in Susan's early teens. At some point she realized that running felt good. It burned away her anger allowing her head to clear. Then she started running even when she wasn't angry. Running became a way for Susan to focus. Emotions melted away and problems would work themselves out in her mind as she ran. Running became Susan's path to enlightenment and now she couldn't imagine life without it.

Gravel popped and crunched under tires as a grey Subaru pulled up the driveway. Susan rose slowly, fighting her growing anticipation. She wanted to bolt down the trails, leaving her thoughts behind her, but that would have to wait. The closer the meet got, the harder the waiting was.

The Subaru crawled up in front of the porch and Susan jumped down to meet it, opening the passenger door, "Are you sure you want to come Anna?"

"Get in already!" Anna rolled her eyes, shifting the car into reverse. "Really, would I have offered to drive if I didn't want to go?"

Susan should have known better than to question Anna's conviction. Still, she couldn't shake the nagging feeling of uncertainty crawling over her skin. Susan needed to get on the track. Now. Throwing her bag in the back seat, Susan climbed in. "Don't get me wrong, I'm glad you're coming! But I don't want to be blamed when you're bored out of your mind and want to go home."

"I won't be bored," Anna reassured her. "I have a bag of film and it's a beautiful day. You might be the one who's bored when you want to go home and I'm still taking pictures."

"It's your funeral," Susan offered one last out, but Anna wasn't biting. "You know, you'd have way more fun if you were participating."

"You would think that." Anna turned her attention to driving. They were finally on their way, heading towards the highway and on to Timber Creek College's trails for the competition. Susan was happy to be on the road and relaxed a little now that everything was in motion.

Once Anna settled into the task of driving she broke through Susan's thoughts. "So... Is Jim going to be there?"

Susan's tongue stuck to the roof of her dry mouth, making it hard to speak. "He said he was coming at practice... but that doesn't mean anything. Jim says a lot of things... doesn't mean he follows up with them."

Anna smiled wryly, "Something tells me he's not going to miss an event that's this important to you."

"Oh please! Don't get my hopes up." The words came out harsher than Susan expected.

"Argh! You're both so dense! It's like two brick walls banging their heads against each other!"

"Walls don't have heads." Susan stuck out her tongue to strengthen her defence. Even bad humour was comforting right now. "You really think he likes me?"

"No, I think he joined a random sports club that you happen to head to get some fresh air and sunshine."

"You're horrible, you know that?"

"Me?!" Anna batted her eyelashes in mock innocence. "Whatever would make you think that?"

Laughter washed away Susan's doubts. Maybe Anna was right and she was working herself up over nothing.

"He likes you," Anna said firmly. "And if he ever breaks your heart, I'll kick his ass."

"Remind me never to make you mad, ever."

"You I could forgive. I don't know about Jim though."

"Aw come on," Susan shifted in her seat, "He's a sweet guy."

"Is he really?"

"Please don't tell me you buy into the rumour mill?" Susan threw her head back into the seat, not wanting to see the disapproving look on her friend's face.

"No," Anna grew quiet. "Considering what the rumour mill has said about me, I don't want to buy anything they're selling. I'm just saying, I want you to be careful. That's all."

"See, the rumour mill doesn't know what they're talking about. You're awesome!"

Anna cringed, tightening her grip on the wheel, but it was impossible to hide from such an obvious compliment. "I hope it doesn't rain. Those clouds don't look so good."

"Don't change the subject! You're amazing and you know it. And I know someone else who knows it!"

Anna's face paled in terror, "Who?"

"Will!"

The edges of Anna's knuckles began to show white. Her mouth pulled into a straight, tight-lipped line. "Can we not talk about him?"

"What is up with you two?!" Susan didn't get it. She needed to understand what was driving Anna's anxiety. "You've been acting weird ever since we started sitting in front of him in Chem. Why?"

"I don't like him, OK."

"Why not? He's a nice guy, way more mature than all of the guys at school put together, smart, not to mention easy on the eyes. What's not to like?"

"I just don't!" Anna yelled.

The hum of the highway intensified in the silence that followed. Anna seldom raised her voice to anyone. Susan had pushed too far, but was no closer to understanding why.

"Look," Anna said as she took a deep breath to calm herself. "I'm sorry, I didn't mean to yell. Will's... not my type OK? I hate that he's always trying to get my attention with his stupid jokes. He thinks he's being funny but he's not. He makes me feel awful. I wish he'd leave me alone."

Realization dawned on Susan as the gravity of the situation sunk in. "I didn't know he was making you feel that way. Why didn't you say something?"

"It's not like I didn't try, but you kept dismissing it as puppy love!" Anna struggled to maintain her composure.

"I'm sorry. I should have listened."

"Well," Anna relented with a sigh, "Sometimes I have a hard time saying things."

"Still, it wasn't my place to tease you or push you when you were really in distress." Susan couldn't believe how blind she had been. "I'm such an idiot!"

"Please don't blame yourself for this."

"Hey, do you want me to talk to him? I'll get him to back off."

"I appreciate the thought Sue, but we aren't in fourth grade anymore. You can't walk up to someone and punch him because he was being mean to me."

"I don't see why not." Susan mulled the idea over. "Some

people could use a good smack upside the head... but that's not what I was getting at. I've refined my persuasion skills over the years to include words you know!"

"Thanks, but I don't know. I'd rather not draw attention to things."

"And how's that working for you?"

"Maybe not as well as I'd like, but give it a chance. Now that you're on board, maybe things will change in a more subtle way."

"Because subtlety is my middle name."

"Don't sell yourself short Sue. Your understanding might be the thing that tips the scales for me."

"If you say so. My offer still stands though."

"Thank you. I mean it."

"Hey, I'll always be there if you need me."

"I know."

They reached the campus. Timber Creek College was its own little world existing within the town, nestled in the heart of civilization, yet sprawling through the natural world around it. The girls drove down the College's roads to the very edge of the campus where the athletic centre opened up to the trails beyond. A small collection of cars filled the tiny parking lot.

"We're not late are we?" Anna scanned the lot for an open space.

"No, but it's going to busy today. We might have to park in the south lot... Nope there's a space! Right at the end!"

The car had barely come to a stop before Susan jumped out, grabbing her bag from the back seat, and jogging off down the path leading to the track where the meet would start.

"Wait up!" Anna scrambled to get her things out of the car.

Susan couldn't stand still and found herself pacing back and forth. She breathed deeply, steadying herself, letting a wave of crisp fall air cool her lungs. She stood at the head of a path lined with birches, their golden leaves falling all around her.

"Ready?" Anna popped up beside her.

"Ready." Susan was surprised at the calm in her voice, but each step forward strengthened her resolve. She was ready. This was her day to shine.

The tarmac below them was misty as steam rose from the pavement baking in the sun. Pale blonde leaves rustled across the track. The facility was simple, a full sized track looped around a field with steel bleachers towering over one side. Behind the bleachers rose a sea of trees containing the trails Susan would navigate during the meet. Open trails on a beautiful fall day. Susan couldn't have asked for anything more.

Waving goodbye to Anna, Susan galloped across the field towards her teammates. The air was full of excitement and nerves, but Susan found their enthusiasm inspiring.

Taking a step out onto the field, Susan collected herself by stretching. Her teammates and coach knew better than to interrupt her while she was preparing for a big run, so it was a surprise when someone jogged up behind her.

"Hey!" Jim panted slightly as if he had run down from the parking lot.

"Hey!" Susan felt suddenly lighter, "Glad you made it before the race started!"

"I said I'd be here!" Jim spread his arms wide presenting himself. "You didn't think I'd miss the big race did you? I'm not going to back down from a competition."

"Even one you're bound to lose?" Susan's competitive streak reared its ugly head, but she was enjoying herself too much to reel it in.

"Ouch! I know I just started with you guys but I'm not that bad am I?"

"No, but if you think you're going to beat me at my own game, think again!"

"Hey, I get it, this is your thing. It's cool. I like the fact that I don't have to hold back around you."

"Why would you hold back? This is a big event for us."

"Yeah well," Jim scratched the back of his head, "With most girls I have to hold back. If I play all out I end up creaming them..."

Susan couldn't take Jim's posturing anymore and the captain in her took over. "Don't do anything to flatter me. Just do your best."

"See, that's what I'm saying I like about you! You can hold your own. I've never met a girl like you before."

"You haven't looked too hard then."

Jim's brows knit together as he struggled to find something to say. "You're hard to complement, you know that?"

Susan stood up from a stretch, about to fling another witty retort, but thought better of it. Maybe Jim was right. She was making this more difficult than it had to be. The ground beneath her feet felt like it was turning to sand and her knees wobbled. "So... um, Jim, are you doing anything next weekend?"

Dimples lit up Jim's face, "Not if you don't want me to!"

"You wanna go see a movie or something?" Susan was dying on the inside, hoping it wouldn't show through her casual exterior.

"A movie? Sure! It's a date!"

Relief flooded Susan's body. "Great! I'll give you my number after the meet. We can sort out the details later."

"Sweet! Susan Wolfe's number!" Jim jumped up, pumping his fist in the air.

"Runners to the start!" The command interrupted their moment of celebration.

It was time. Jim was a pleasant distraction, but now Susan had to focus on what she came here to do. The jitters in her legs ceased. Susan threw Jim some incentive, "Well, maybe I'll give my number to you if you can keep up!"

She didn't wait for a response but bounded off toward the start.

Susan jostled through the crowd, trying to grab a spot near the front of the pack. When the gun went off, she didn't want anyone in her way. Adrenaline from asking Jim out surged in her veins and she could hear the blood already pounding in her ears. Her body felt like it was on fire. She needed to run.

The open field stretched before them, long grass waving in the breeze. At the end of the field, a marked trail beckoned to the runners. A hush fell over the crowd as they were called to the mark.

The gunshot pierced the silence, and Susan flew forward. Cheers and her coach's screams about pacing faded into the background. The thunder of the other runners feet fell behind her as Susan broke free from the emotions that were binding her. The delicious fall air filled her lungs and her muscles sang with release.

The opening burst was short and sweet. It felt good to let out everything pent up from her encounter with Jim, but after that moment, Susan remembered the race. As good as it felt to sprint through the opening, it wouldn't help her in the long run. As she reached the mouth of the trail Susan forced her legs to slow and she set a pace for herself. Falling into a steady rhythm, her feet pounded along the hard packed earth. Other runners would pass her or fall back and Susan kept an eye on them, concentrating on her pace. Her world became her breathing, and the contours of the trail.

The terrain was challenging. Fresh fallen leaves littered the ground, still damp and glistening. The sun's rays spat through the branches, but the clouds that had been threatening earlier rolled in. The light on the trail defused, becoming grey and hazy as the race wore on.

As she ran, Susan's thoughts began to untangle. Her heart hammered away over Jim, allowing her mind the room it needed to unravel and weave new patterns. She still couldn't believe she had asked him out, or that he had said yes. A world of possibilities opened up before her and everything fell into place. The outside world melted away until there was only Susan and the trail she was conquering. The joy of running coursed through her with every step.

Then the path opened up exposing the track and bleachers. The foreign sound of people and the smell of the synthetic track assaulted Susan's nose as the outside world rushed back into her brain. She wanted to veer off into the bush again, back to the state of bliss she was so rudely ejected from. However, the goal of the finish line flashed before Susan's eyes and her need to cross it blazed anew. The end was in sight. It was all or nothing.

Susan forgot her aching muscles, and calculated breathing, letting loose her last reserves. She bolted forward with everything she had, flying past the other runners. The noise of the crowd peaked as Susan crossed the finish. Mission accomplished. She gulped for air through ragged breaths and her body slowed, then stopped altogether. Her knees felt weak, and her head was swimming, but her runner's high bathed her body in euphoria. It took a moment for her coach's words to penetrate her ears.

"... your best time Wolfe! First place! I knew you could do it!"

"Good... that's good." Susan panted. She would celebrate later. Right now she was still in the zone running had put her in and she wanted to stay there as long as she could.

"With that crazy start I thought you were going to burn yourself out before the race was half over! I don't know where you keep all that energy, but it looks like it worked out for you in the end."

"Yeah... thanks." Susan resumed walking around the track giving her muscles a chance to cool down. People came by to congratulate her, but she shrugged off the praise.

It felt good simply to have run the race and Susan wanted to enjoy that high while it lasted.

Eventually Anna walked up beside her. She didn't say anything, just followed Susan around the track.

"That was amazing," Susan said signalling she was ready to talk.

"I'll say!" Anna's eyes shone in amazement. "I've never seen you run so fast before! It's almost like you had a little extra something to keep you going today."

"Huh, what?" Anna was hinting at something, but Susan's mind was still coming back down to earth.

"You know, something tall dark and handsome that might have given you a little energy spurt before the race?"

The pieces clicked and Susan grew excited again. "I asked Jim out!"

"What?! Are you serious?! I thought something was going on, but I thought he was putting the moves on you!"

"He tried. It was adorable, but kind of painful, so I decided to bite the bullet and ask him instead."

"Well look at you!" Anna took a step back, examining Susan in wonder.

"Today must be my lucky day."

"You have to tell me everything! Right now!"

"I would but I gotta go shower, maybe receive a medal or something."

"Oh come on! You can't take a minute to give your best friend all the gory details?"

"Come over for dinner! I'll give you all the gory details you want!" Susan was already backing off toward the finish line. Anna protested, but would have to wait, at least until the car ride home. Then they could gush all they wanted. Right now Susan had other priorities to her team and her sport. A drop of rain hit Susan's face and she looked up at the blackening sky. Of course life had to rain on her parade.

CHAPTER 4
DATE

Susan practically vibrated with excitement. She was going on a date with Jim Schenn. She couldn't believe she had asked him out. More unbelievable still, he had said yes. Susan called in Anna for an emergency consultation to help her prepare for the big night. She could barely function as it was, so it was a relief to have Anna around to help her pick out clothes and keep her from bouncing off the walls.

Susan stood in front of the bathroom mirror trying to tame her unruly mane, while Anna sat on the edge of the tub, staring off into space.

"What's up with you today?" Susan glanced at her friend's reflection in the mirror.

"I dunno..." Anna said, studying the tiles of the bathroom floor.

"Oh no, don't do this to me now!"

"What?" Anna looked up, innocence shining in her eyes.

"That thing you do when something's on your mind! You get all quiet and evasive instead of talking about it. It drives me crazy!"

"I do what now?"

"Great, you don't even know you're doing it!" Susan wanted to bang her head against her reflection.

"Sorry, I know you're stressed out about your date..." Anna grew quiet and trailed off.

"There! You're doing it again!" Susan spun around leaning her back against the counter.

Anna bit her lip, avoiding eye contact.

Susan sighed, "I can't help if you won't tell me about it."

"I... I know," Anna slumped forward. "Don't get me wrong, I'm happy things are working out for you with Jim but... maybe I'm a little jealous."

Susan's heart sank into her stomach. "Why didn't you say something?"

"Are you kidding? I wasn't going to ruin this for you."

"You're too sensitive for your on good, you know that?"

"Tell me about it." Anna's shoulders drooped.

Susan couldn't shake the feeling that there was more to this than a twinge of jealousy. "Are you sure you're OK?"

Anna rose from the tub, grabbed a hair brush from the counter and proceeded to dismantle Susan's attempt at hairstyling. "You should wear it down. It looks best that way."

"But it doesn't feel special *au natural.*"

"Don't worry, you're plenty special!" Anna couldn't help the dry edge to her words.

Susan stood patiently while Anna brushed her hair. "We'll talk about it tomorrow then."

"About what?" Anna's oblivious streak continued, proving to Susan that her mind was occupied elsewhere.

"Whatever it is that's eating you. Don't think you can get away so easily! I might be a little distracted tonight, but I've got all day tomorrow to spend with you."

"Do you really think we're going to talk about me after your big date?" Anna smoothed out a stray lick of hair.

"We'll make time. I promise." Susan waved away Anna's fussing hands, running her fingers though her hair giving it one last comb. "I hate it when you're right. It looks so much better this way."

"Tomorrow," Anna held the brush close to her chest, running her fingers over the bristles. "Don't forget."

"I won't. Come over and we'll sort everything out."

"OK," Anna said meekly, but a quiet resolve grew across her face.

"Sue! Your ride's here!" Her mother called from the hallway.

Panic surged through Susan. She wasn't ready. She would never be ready. She wanted to run down the hall and possibly straight out the door and down the street, but she urged herself to relax and walk to the door. Her legs wobbled beneath her, and her head felt light. She had to double check to make sure she had everything.

"He's not going to come in and say hi?" Mrs. Wolfe peeked out the window to inspect the boy who would spirit away her daughter for the evening.

"Mom, please don't drag this out!" Susan's heart began to race. This was not the time to be arguing with her mother.

"Fine," Mrs. Wolfe backed away from the window. "Just make sure you're home by eleven."

"Eleven?!" Susan screeched. "What am I, a kid?"

The two Wolfes stood facing one another, each weighing the other carefully.

"Eleven-thirty then," her mother said.

"Twelve."

Mrs. Wolfe grew stern, the edges of her mouth twitching the way they did when she was annoyed. She wasn't going to back down anytime soon and every minute they stood arguing was a minute less Susan had to spend with Jim.

"Fine, eleven-thirty! Don't wait up!" Susan nearly pulled the door off its hinges on her way out, before racing down the driveway to Jim's car. Jumping into the passenger seat her first words to Jim were, "Let's go!"

"You're pretty excited! It's just a movie." Despite his

casual tone, Jim's face lit up as he watched Susan buckle herself in.

"Yeah but I'm going with you!" Susan kicked herself. She probably shouldn't be so obvious. "I mean, movies drastically improve if the company is cute."

"So I'm cute am I?" Jim pulled out of the driveway, turning down the road to head to the highway.

Susan wanted to scream for digging herself in deeper. She paused a moment to collect herself, letting Jim's question slide while forcing herself to calm down and act normal. "So, which movie did you want to see?"

"Oh yeah, I hope you don't mind, but I printed out some tickets already. I remember you saying your mom was a bit of a ..." Jim coughed, "Stickler, so I wanted to make sure we could get into an early show."

"You thought that far ahead?" Susan asked, impressed.

"Um, Yeah." Jim brushed his fingers distractedly through his hair.

Not only had Jim been on time for their date, but he had planned ahead. Susan's brain went mushy as her thoughts blurred and her cheeks grew warm. "Oh yeah, I kind of have a curfew."

"What's the damage?"

"Eleven-thirty." Susan wanted to crawl into a hole. She felt like the only girl in Timber Creek whose Mom would actually enforce such a ridiculous restriction.

"Ouch!" Jim winced dramatically. "Don't worry, we'll have plenty of time to hang out, thanks to my quick thinking!"

"You win this round," Susan threw Jim some praise. "So what movie are we seeing?"

"The tickets are on the dash," Jim pointed.

Susan grabbed the papers. When she saw the title, her heart dropped, "A romantic comedy?"

"I tried to pick something you'd like. We could always pick something else when we get there."

"No it's fine!" It didn't matter what they saw, the important thing was that Jim had thought of her and that she got to spend time with him.

"Sorry, I should have asked what you wanted to see."

"No really, don't worry about it! I'm sure I'll live."

Jim let out a sigh of relief. "You're easy to be around, you know that?"

"You're not the first person to tell me that, so it must be true."

Jim took a hand off the wheel and reached for one of Susan's. Their fingers naturally wove together as if they'd done so many times before. It was comfortable. Susan relaxed, enjoying the warmth of Jim's hand.

The drive flew by and it wasn't long before they were surrounded by the smell of buttered popcorn and the darkness of the theatre. Susan's instincts had been right, the movie was terrible, but at least they could laugh together at how bad it was. With anyone else, Susan might have been miserable, but the fact that Jim was willing to sacrifice his ego at the altar of humor won her over completely. They sat together laughing all the way through the credits, even as the lights came on and the attendants waited for the theatre to empty. Grudgingly they left their seats and strolled out toward the exit.

"I'm sorry you had to sit through that," Jim said.

"It wasn't that bad!"

"Are you kidding me?"

"Alright, it was bad, but I still had fun watching it with you."

Jim swaggered a little with satisfaction, "You're pretty fun yourself."

Susan checked the time on her phone. "It's still early. Do you want to go for a coffee or something?"

"Actually," Jim slowed, carefully weighing his words. "I was thinking... There's this place up by Old Mill Road that's got a killer view. If you want, I can show it to you."

Susan's mind began to spin. Jim was offering to take her somewhere special and probably private. Old Mill Road wasn't exactly the hub of civilization. "What's up there to see in the dark?"

"It wouldn't be a surprise if I told you."

Susan weighed her intrigue against the voice of responsibility nagging in her head. The prospect of being alone with Jim was too enticing to pass up, however she hesitated, "I dunno..."

"It's not far. I promise we won't get you home too late."

That tiny bit of rebellion pushed Susan over the edge. "Let's go!"

It was already dark outside and the air was getting colder, but at least the night was clear. As they drove away from the glow of town, the patterns of stars across the sky became more pronounced. The traffic lessened as they went down more remote roads and the night swallowed up anything outside the car's headlights. Susan would never have noticed the little side road they turned down. At least Jim was confident where they were going. The road turned into a dirt trail and eventually ended at a line of trees. Jim pulled the car to the side of the trail, parking on the shoulder.

Jim leaned over, enticingly close to Susan. "I hope you're up for a bit of a walk."

Jim's scent flooded Susan's nose, arousing something feral deep within her. "I'm game if you are!" She kicked the car door open, jumping out into the chill fall night.

The bush was serene and still around them. A few leaves shivered on the trees, but for the most part, it was quiet. The full moon cast a silvery sheen on the trees making grey branches stand out against shadows that wavered in the dark. Even the scent of wet leaves had a silvery tang to it. It was like a dream, all too real, but hazy around the edges.

"It's this way." Jim led them to the opening of a foot path that wound uphill. Leaves crunched underfoot, echoing through the bush as they wove their way up the trail. The trees thinned and opened to a ridge overlooking the town. The lights of Timber Creek pushed against the darkness of the surrounding bush, weaving a glowing haven out of the wilderness.

"It's beautiful!" Susan drank in the view, more than willing to lose herself in the sight.

"Yeah, you'd never think this town could be beautiful, but sometimes you just need to know where to look."

Susan recognized the spite and hope in Jim's voice. Timber Creek could be isolating and cold, but at the same time, that was its beauty. Out here she could be wild and free, but only within the limits the town had to offer.

"Are you cold?" Jim asked as his arm wrapped around her shoulders.

"A little," Susan shivered, but couldn't tell if it was from the cold or Jim's touch. They snuggled into one another for warmth. The lights of the town dimmed and blurred as Susan's attention focused on something new. Jim's dark, rich scent surrounded her, making her lightheaded. She allowed the sensation to seep into her body. A tiny spark of fear leapt inside her, but excitement drowned it out as she found her face lifting toward Jim's.

He was watching her and as she gazed up at him, his lips came down to connect with hers. The heat from his raw mouth seeped into Susan and spread through her core like fire. Her body moved on its own accord, grabbing Jim's waist and pulling him closer. He responded by wrapping his arms tightly around her. Susan let the fire burn a swath of bliss through her as their kiss deepened. She let her mind go the way it did when she ran, allowing her body to focus on the moment.

Despite the blissful heat, a growl formed in the pit of Susan's stomach. She broke off the kiss, drawing in a sharp breath of cold air. Jim hovered over her, his hands still gripping her waist. Susan took a few more deep breaths, but the strange feeling of unease had gone. She returned to Jim's lips with gusto.

The pair stood on the ridge, awash in silver moonlight, warmed by the distant glow of the town. Jim's hands roved over Susan's body. At first it was a little alarming, but eventually she became comfortable with Jim's advances. Cold fingers brushed against the skin of her waist as they reached inside her coat, tugging at the edge of her shirt. The uneasy growl returned, this time rolling up and over her in a wave of panic.

Susan took a step back. "Whoa! Easy there tiger."

Jim looked confused. "Sorry, I thought you were enjoying yourself."

"I am. I mean I was. No, I... it's..." Susan couldn't explain something she wasn't sure of herself. Why had she shut her brain off when she needed it most? The disquiet growl still rumbled through her, ricocheting through her body. "I'm not sure I feel so well. Maybe we should stop."

Susan veered away from Jim, attempting to scout out the trail that lead back to the car, but he caught her arm. "What's wrong? I thought you liked me?"

"I do!" The inner growl rose, pounding in her eardrums, but Susan forced herself to ignore it. Placing her hand over Jim's, she reassured him. "I do like you Jim, and I want to do this again, but right now, I think I should go home." She couldn't control the uncertain waver in her voice.

Jim called her on it. "You don't sound too sure. If this is about your mom, I promise to bail you out if she freaks. Can't we have just a little more time together?"

Susan melted from Jim's charm. She did want to stay, but something wasn't right. The rumble inside her wouldn't go away, no matter how much she willed it down or ignored it. Maybe she was sick, maybe her nerves were getting to her, but either way, Susan knew she was finished and needed to go home. "It's not that. I can deal with my mom."

"Well, what is it then? Come on," His voice deepened as he drew closer to her body. "I really like you Sue."

Susan begin to tremble. The growl inside her expanded, clawing out from the pit of her stomach, toward her chest. It seized her heart, pounding in time with its rhythm. She felt warm as a new fire blazed through her body. It took all of Susan's strength to remain focused on her conversation with Jim. "I need to go home." She tried to take a step back, but Jim held her firmly in place.

"I know you're probably nervous, but there's nothing to be scared about. I promise!" He dragged her shaking body back into an embrace, clamping another iron-solid arm around her waist. "You must be nervous, you're shivering."

Susan was anxious, but Jim wasn't helping. The more she tried to control the trembling the less she seemed to be able to move. Terror gripped her as she realized her body wasn't responding to her thoughts. The fire entered her brain and she struggled to think. Through force of will, she had a single moment of clarity when she tried to push herself out of Jim's arms. Unfortunately her arms barely twitched and the scream inside her head came out as a whisper, "No."

"It'll be alright. I promise." He kissed her again, holding her tightly. What was once a secure embrace was now a prison.

A chill of fear doused the burning in Susan's chest and once again she was aware that something was desperately wrong. Jim didn't understand that she was in distress and her body was somehow detached from her mind, functioning on its own accord. This couldn't be happening. It couldn't be real. Susan wanted to scream, but all that came out was a weak movement of her lips, her words having no voice to back them. Terror twisted Susan's insides. She wished with all her might that everything would stop. But the panic that wildly tore at her heart began to take shape. There was something familiar, almost comforting, about it. Instead of fighting the fire, Susan let it in.

The flames roared to life and the deep growl bellowed a thunderous howl. Her body ripped apart, torn inside-out, flesh melted and plied into new shapes. Her brain felt too small for her skull as if it would burst through the bone scattering shards in its wake.

Then everything stopped and the world around Susan was crystal clear. The burning was gone, there was no pain or uncertainty. The night was alive with sounds and smells, however, danger was standing right before her. Fear prickled the hair on the back of her neck as she remembered that someone was holding her against her will. He was going to hurt her if she didn't escape.

Susan didn't think, she reacted. Her assailant's eyes went wide and he smelled of fear. Her lips drew back and she lunged forward, sinking her teeth into her captor's neck. Her jaws clamped down on the soft tissue, and Susan was rewarded with the warm, coppery taste of blood gushing into her mouth. The momentum of her attack pushed them over backwards. Susan refused to let go, even as they tumbled down the hill. Slamming into a tree, forced her jaws open with a yelp.

She had to get up. The danger might still be there ready to harm her. Clawing at the ground Susan struggled to rise, but couldn't find her balance. Everything was wrong. Her muscles weren't responding the way they should. Panic rose in her throat. *What's wrong with me?!* She looked down at her hands trying to piece the puzzle together and was shocked to see a pair of paws in their place.

Susan recoiled, but as she jumped back, the paws went with her. Tentatively she lifted what should have been her right hand and the paw respond in kind. *What the hell is going on?*

A gurgling noise choked through the hush of the trees and the air thickened with the scent of blood. Susan whirled to face a body lying a few feet beside her. It twitched, thrashing in the bushes as it lay bleeding through its mangled throat. The fear pumping through Susan's body went ice cold when she recognized the dark scent surfacing through the carnage. Danger and the boy she cared for were one and the same. It didn't make sense. Susan struggled to reconcile the two powerful feelings inside her. In the end, compassion won and her actions took on a whole new meaning. Horror over what she had done tore through her. She wanted to scream, but all that came out was a howl.

Susan let pain sweep through her, but this time the inner growl receded, cowed into submission by her guilt. "No," her words rang human again. "No, this isn't happening. Jim!"

Tears stung her eyes as she stumbled forward. Jim struggled to breathe, the torn flesh of his throat dangling to one side. His skin looked ashen, but then everything looked grey in the moonlight. Susan flushed with nausea and retched into the bushes. Sucking in deep breaths of air, she lifted a hand to wipe away the bile. Her face felt wet and tacky. As she pulled her hand away, the moonlight reveled the dark, glistening blood she had wiped from her face. Susan wanted to vomit again, but couldn't seem to move. Her fingers trembled as she realized the taste of blood on her mouth came from Jim.

Susan tore off her coat rubbing her face down, as if it might remove the things she had done. But it couldn't wash away her sin. Jim was dying because of her. *Dying... he's not dead yet.*

Susan bunched up her coat, placing it over the wound in Jim's throat and pressing down to staunch the flow of blood. "It's OK, I'm here! I'm not going to let you die Jim!"

Air rattled out of Jim's throat, but his eyes began to dim.

"Dammit Jim, don't give up on me! Don't let go!" The trembling in Susan's fingers moved up to her arms. Jim was dying and they were out in the middle of nowhere. Worst of all it was her fault. Susan had done this to him.

"No... not yet." Her mind flashed to her purse, sitting in the car, her cell phone tucked inside. "Jim, listen to me, I'm going to get my phone. I'm going to call 911. I'll come straight back, I promise."

Jim didn't respond to indicate he had heard or understood what she said, but there wasn't a moment to lose. Susan wouldn't allow her guilt to hold her back a second longer. That second might make all the difference.

Susan flew down the hill, running, falling, and picking herself up again. It didn't matter as long as she kept moving toward the car. Panic forced her to gasp for air and the stench of Jim's blood stuck in her lungs making it hard to breathe. Branches slapped her as she ran through the brush, but Susan couldn't afford to let anything hold her back.

At last, the car came into view. Susan didn't slow down, ramming herself into the hood to stop. Her entire body shook when she pushed herself back, revealing two dark handprints on the metal. Susan tried to swallow, but her throat tightened. She spat out the offending bile and clenched her hands into fists.

"Calm down, calm down..." she repeated the mantra until her breathing became more controlled. She couldn't help anyone if she kept freaking out.

Lights flashed and the rumble of an engine echoed down the road. The noise cut through the pounding rush of blood in Susan's ears and she looked up to see a truck approaching. She needed help. Staggering onto the road, Susan waved down the truck. It pulled up beside her and the driver swung himself out and down to the ground.

"Damn kids! You know this is private prop..."

Susan jumped at the man. "Help! Please, we need help!"

The driver examined her in the glare of the headlights, taking a step back, realizing her torn clothes were soaked in blood. "Jesus Christ! What happened?"

"Please..." Susan croaked.

The truck door slammed shut and another man appeared beside the first. "What's wrong? Are you hurt?"

Susan wanted to cry. "No! It's Jim... h... he's hurt. He might be dying!"

"Where's your friend?" The second man kept his voice calm.

A light flickered from the cab of the truck and the driver shone a flashlight into the trees. Susan wasted no time explaining, leading them back into the woods. Despite her chaotic trip down the hill, she knew where they needed to go. The bush seemed darker in the presence of the flashlight, and the shadows it cast, made everything look unfamiliar. Susan lost sense of where they were. She called out, hoping Jim could make a noise that might reorient them, but only silence answered.

"Jim! JIM!" Susan's cries intensified, until a bright patch of crimson lit up in the flashlight's wake. "Jim!" A beat of relief escaped her heart as she rushed toward him. However, fear seized her muscles as she approached. Something was wrong. Jim was stone still, his unmoving eyes staring at something just out of reach.

"Move." The calmer man commanded, but Susan's body didn't respond. She stepped to the side as he nudged her out of the way. Bending down over Jim, he examined the throat before grabbing Jim's wrist, holding two fingers over the pulse. His face was grim as he balled one hand into a fist, placing the other overtop and began pushing down on the boy's chest with rhythm. Despite the cold air, sweat beaded on his brow. After a few repeated attempts at checking and pushing, the man slumped down on the forest floor, defeated.

Susan couldn't believe it. She couldn't give up. Kneeling beside Jim, she went to check the wound in his neck, but drew back when her fingers touched the cold flesh. Jim was dead.

The world swam in and out of Susan's vision, pushing her away from her senses until she felt like she was watching everything from far away. Voices blurred into unidentifiable noise. She knew when she was moving, but couldn't feel the ground beneath her. Her vision swam in and out of a haze. She was aware of people arriving, but couldn't tell how long they'd been there. It was as if they were popping up out of the ground. The flashing sirens hurt her head, but eventually she tuned them out as well. She surrendered silently to the paramedics, hoping they could stop the whirlwind she saw every time she closed her eyes. Everything happened wretchedly slow, but then the moment would spin quickly by, hard to recall.

After a while, voices began to separate and her surroundings solidified.

"...she hasn't said a word."

"Might be a while yet. She's had quite a shock."

"What got the boy? Any word about that yet?"

"Coroner hasn't committed to anything, but I think it's obvious."

Susan stiffened. They already knew.

"What do you think got him? A bear?"

"Probably. Wolves are pretty rare around here."

"But not unheard of..."

Confusion rattled around what was left of Susan's working brain. She was the one who had killed Jim, not some stupid bear or wolf.

Wolf. The word jarred her mind. It had been her. She was the wolf. She was the animal that they were looking for. The hairs on the back of her neck stood on end and her posture straightened as an urge to run gnawed at her legs. The shift in posture did not go unnoticed however, and a man approached – a police officer.

"Hi there, how are you feeling?" He crouched down in front of her, his voice and expression soft.

Susan made an effort to swallow. She opened her mouth to say something, but couldn't find the words. Instead she curled forward and let out a sob as tears welled in her eyes.

The officer continued to speak quietly and sat beside her on the ambulance tail gate. "It's alright, you're safe now. Nothing is going to hurt you."

Susan choked at the irony of his words and continued to bawl. She didn't want to stop. It was her fault. Jim was dead and she was the one who killed him. She turned into a wolf and bit him. No, that was insane. There's no way she could have done that even if she wanted to. This had to be a dream, the world's most horrible nightmare. Susan cried for a while, until her sobs went dry. She couldn't force out another tear if she tried.

A warm, rich smell comforted her nose. The officer held out a *Tim's* cup. "It's hot chocolate. It'll make you feel better."

Susan automatically reached out taking the paper cup from him. They must have been waiting for a while as the cup wasn't its usual scalding self. She nodded her thanks, holding the cup in her lap, letting it warm her hands.

"How are you feeling?"

"T... terrible." Her voice cracked. It sounded weak and foreign, but at least it was working.

"Well, you were in shock. What's your name?"

"Susan Wolfe."

"OK, Ms Wolfe, do you know where you are?"

"Not really. The middle of nowhere."

"Fair enough, how about what day it is?"

"Friday," The word swam up through the fog. "It's Friday night, or maybe it's Saturday by now." Something clicked, "Mom! I should have been back by now, she's probably freaking out! She doesn't know where I am!"

"Take it easy," The officer held up a hand. "Why don't you tell me your number and I'll give her a call to tell her you're alright?"

It needed to be done so Susan recited her home number and the officer left to make the call. Susan took the opportunity to check her surroundings and was startled to find the man from the truck standing nearby, watching her. He hesitated before approaching her. "Ah... are you OK miss?"

Susan hung her head. Other people's concern for her wellbeing drove the icy wedge of guilt deeper into her heart. "I'm fine."

"You scared us half to death when you jumped out like that!"

Susan wanted to tell him to go away. The last thing she wanted was anyone's sympathy.

"Look I'm sorry about what happened," The man took a step back, "I just wanted to make sure you were alright."

"You didn't have to wait around just for me."

"Well, I've been busy with the cops and everything too, but they've got my name and statement so I should probably get going."

A chill crawled up Susan's spine. The police. The officer would be back and he was going to ask her questions. What was she going to say?

"Thanks. I'll be alright." Susan tried to make her smile convincing, even though her insides were screaming. Thankfully, it seemed to do the trick and the man from the truck went on his way.

The officer returned, taking a seat on the tailgate again, but this time flipping open a pad of paper and taking out the pen attached to its side. "I talked to your mom, so she knows you're alright. I'll bring you home, but I'd like to ask you a couple of questions first?"

Here we go. Susan buried her attention in her hot chocolate. It was colder than she would have liked, but the liquid still burned her dry throat on the way down. "Shoot."

"I'd like you tell me what happened. Take your time."

"I... I don't really know."

"Why don't you start at the beginning, when you came out here?"

"Right. We were on a date. We went to see a movie." Susan snorted. It was all so mundane. "It was kind of bad, the movie, but we had a fun time. Anyway, after the movie we wanted to hang out more and Jim said he wanted to show me this place." Susan gestured to the hill. "He took me up to the ridge where you can see the lights. It was so beautiful..." Susan faltered, unsure how to continue. The truth sounded ludicrous.

"What happened next?" The officer prodded gently.

Raising the *Tim's* cup to her lips, Susan drained the last of her hot chocolate. "Jim... Jim said he had to take a leek, so he went off into the trees. I heard noises, but I thought it was Jim walking through the bush." Images rushed back to her in vivid clarity. "I think he screamed... no I'm not sure. It all happened so fast. One minute we were standing together on the ridge and the next thing I know we're halfway down the hill. I... I must have tripped or something."

"So, you heard noises and Jim sounded like he was in distress?"

"Yes."

"When you heard the noises what did you do?"

"I don't know. I only remember falling. I..."

"Take a deep breath and think."

Susan paused to collect her thoughts. She wanted to tell the officer what made the most sense. She didn't want to lie to him, but the truth was so much harder to tell. "I went towards him. I lost my footing and fell down the hill."

"Are you sure?"

Last chance. "Yes. I fell down the hill and landed near Jim. I was scared. I didn't know what was happening. Then I realized Jim was hurt. He was bleeding... there was blood all over..." Susan paused again, but bit back her fear. "I tried to help him. I took my coat and tried to stop the bleeding. I... I might have puked in the bushes first though. Then I remembered my cell phone was back in the car. I didn't want to leave him, but I didn't know what else to do. So I ran to the car. That's when the men in the truck came. They helped me look for Jim, but by the time we found him..."

Susan dug her fingernails into her palms hard enough to elicit some pain. "The one man, not the driver, the other one... I didn't get his name... he tried CPR, but it was no use. Jim was dead when we found him. I wanted to help him, but when I touched his skin it... it was cold." Susan wanted to curl up and cry again, but all she could do was sit there and shiver.

"Susan, I'm going to read my notes back to you and you tell me if there's anything I need to add or change."

"That's it? Really?" Doubts nagged at her. Would she get away with these lies and half truths? Should she? Exhaustion seeped into Susan's body. "I'm so tired," she confessed.

"Don't worry, it's all over now. You're safe."

"I'm not the one I'm worried about."

"I know. I'm sorry for your loss."

Clutching her knees to her chest, Susan shuddered as fresh tears streamed down her face. She mumbled into her jeans, torn between hoping the officer could hear her and hoping that he couldn't. "I'm sorry... so sorry... oh God, Jim, I'm so sorry!"

CHAPTER 5
CONFESSIONS

The wind bit through Anna's thin jacket as she stepped from her car onto Susan's driveway. The beautiful weather they had been having was now threatened by grey skies and the chill of winter. Anna shivered, pulling up the jacket's collar around her ears as she scuttled towards the house.

As she approached the door, Anna became unsettled by the silence surrounding her. She expected to hear Susan and her mother, or Susan's rambunctious little brother Ben making a commotion, but the normally bustling house was still. Even the wind outside had died.

Anna lifted her hand to knock, but the door creaked open on its own, revealing a miserable looking Mrs. Wolfe. "Oh Anna! I'm glad you're here!" she said rubbing bleary, red eyes.

Anna's heart leapt into her throat. "What... what's wrong? What happened?!"

"Oh! I'm sorry, I didn't mean to scare you! I must look like such a mess."

It was hard not to be frightened. Mrs. Wolfe looked as if she'd been up half the night crying. "What's going on? Is Sue OK?"

"Yes... yes Susan's alright... mostly..."

"What do you mean?!"

"Wow, I'm really bad at this! Let me start from the beginning. Susan is fine, but... there was an accident last night Anna, and... it's Jim. He didn't make it."

Anna's heart dropped from her throat to the pit of her stomach. She felt ill. "No, is he... he can't be."

"I'm sorry. Let's get you out of the cold." A hand on her shoulder pulled her inside.

Anna obeyed, allowing herself to be lead to the couch in the living room. She felt stiff as if all the muscles in her body had tensed at once. "So... he's... Jim's dead?" The idea flew through her mind, hard to grasp.

"Yes." Mrs. Wolfe sat down beside her.

Tears came unbidden. Everything felt surreal. "And Sue? You said she's alright. Is she hurt at all?"

Mrs. Wolfe placed a reassuring hand on Anna's. "She's not hurt, not physically anyway. She went into shock last night, but by the time she made it home, she was recovering from that. The paramedics said she'd be alright, it's just... she *found* him Anna."

"What do you mean?"

"Right, I didn't tell you about the accident." Mrs. Wolfe took a deep breath, steadying herself. "Apparently Susan and Jim decided to go off on a little adventure after the movie, up Old Mill Road. They were out in the middle of nowhere and Jim was attacked by some kind of wild animal. Susan didn't see what happened but... she found Jim after he'd been attacked." Mrs. Wolfe cleared her throat. "She tried to save him, but Jim didn't make it."

They sat in silence for a moment on the couch before Anna leaned forward and began to sob. She had a hard time believing this was real, yet her body reacted accordingly and she let herself cry. Mrs. Wolfe sat with her, holding her hand until the crying subsided.

"I understand if you want to go home," Mrs. Wolfe tugged at Anna's hand, "But if you're up to it, I think Susan could really use a good friend right now."

Anna nodded. Her throat felt raw as she spoke, "I'd like to see her."

"I'll see if she's awake." Mrs. Wolfe rose and padded down the hallway.

Anna realized her hands where shaking. She tried to steady them, but the trembling only moved up to her arms. She closed her eyes, trying to calm down.

"She's awake if you want to see her. I don't think she slept much though." Worry creased Mrs. Wolfe's face making her look much older than she was. Susan wasn't the only person who hadn't slept the night before.

Anna walked past Mrs. Wolfe and down the hall. The door to Susan's room was ajar. She pushed it open. Susan was sitting on her bed, hugging her knees to her chest. Her hair, normally a vibrant, sunny gold, looked dark and lifeless as it hung limp over her face. Her pallid skin emphasized the dark circles under her eyes. When she saw Anna at the door, her lips, which were tightly pressed together, broke open as if she was trying to speak, but no words came out.

Anna rushed to Susan's side, wrapping her arms around her. "It's OK Sue. It's going to be OK!"

Susan hugged Anna back, crying into her shoulder. Through sobs Susan choked out, "It's not OK! It's NOT!" Then she shoved Anna away, and hid her face behind her hands.

Anna was shaken, unsure what to say. "I'm sorry Sue. I... I don't know what you're going through right now, but I'm here if you want to talk... or if you don't. It doesn't matter. If you want me to go home, I can..."

"No! Stay!" Susan grabbed Anna's wrist pulling her to sit on the bed next to her. "Please stay. Don't go."

"I'm not going anywhere." Anna freed her wrist from

Susan's death grip, gently taking her friend's hand in hers. She studied Susan's worried face, searching for something reassuring to say. "You look awful."

"Hah," Susan's laugh was harsh. "I should!"

Anna waited a moment before asking, "What happened?"

Susan tensed as if she might break down again, but instead returned to clutching her knees to her chest. "I don't know. It was such a mess. I... Jim..." Susan broke off, staring Anna squarely in the eye. "Anna, I have to tell someone. I lied last night! I wanted to tell the truth, but I was afraid... so afraid. It doesn't make any sense, no matter how many times I go over it in my head. It doesn't make sense!"

"These things don't make sense Sue..."

"That's not what I mean!" Anger flashed across Susan's face but it was quickly replaced with fear. "Please, I need to tell someone the truth. It's going to sound crazy, even I know that. That's why I couldn't say it before, but if I don't tell someone the truth, I might explode."

"I'm listening." Anna pulled up her legs onto the bed sitting quietly across from Susan.

"Promise me you won't tell anyone." The glint of fear shone wild in Susan's eyes.

"You know I won't..."

"This is different Anna. I... I'm afraid." A shudder ran through Susan's body.

"Whatever it is, you can tell me, then we'll figure out where to go from there together."

"Yeah," Susan relaxed, letting go of her knees, folding her legs in front of her. "What did my Mom tell you exactly?"

"She said there was an accident, some kind of animal attacked Jim, and that you tried to save him but he didn't make it."

"That's what they all think." Susan rubbed her temples. "It's true, except I left out the most important part."

Anna waited, while Susan collected her thoughts.

Susan started to speak a couple of times, but couldn't get the words out. Finally she said, "It's my fault Jim's dead."

"You can't think that way. It was an accident…"

"Yeah, it was, but I was the one who attacked him. I killed Jim."

Anna's head swam. Susan wasn't making sense. Maybe the stress of the previous night was making her friend delusional.

"You think I'm nuts right? Or I'm lying, but it's the truth, the honest to God truth."

"How…"

Susan froze staring Anna squarely in the eye. "I turned into a wolf and bit Jim. I don't know how, but it must have happened because Jim's dead and they said an animal tore out his neck. I saw it myself. There was blood… everywhere."

"Sue, you went through something horrible last night."

"And you think I'm crazy."

"No, I think what you experienced was very real to you, but there has to be some rational explanation!" Anna's anxiety rose. She could be as patient and understanding as possible, but she wasn't equipped to deal with this kind of trauma. She was in way over her head. "It's going to be OK Sue, we'll figure this out."

"Dammit! I knew you wouldn't get it!" Susan threw up her hands before crossing them defiantly in front of her chest.

Guilt squeezed Anna's heart. She had always been there for Susan, and right now she was trying to understand, but Susan's accusation burned. "Maybe I should go."

As Anna rose from the bed, Susan lunged forward, but the shape of her body warped like a mirage. Susan collapsed on the bed, twitching and struggling against an unseen force. Anna froze, rooted to the floor. Susan spasmed a few times and the warping intensified as her body morphed into an animal. Curious green-gold eyes peeked over the rumpled sheets of the bed. Anna found herself face to face with a wolf, its fur the same tawny colour as Susan's hair. Susan's pajamas hung awkwardly on its body. It grinned at her, panting from exertion.

Anna couldn't move. Her mouth had gone dry, but a single word managed to rasp its way out, "Sue?"

The wolf bobbed its head up and down.

Anna took a step, slowly moving toward the wolf, waiting for it to jump out and bite her, but it sat where it was, panting. Anna reached out her hand. They both flinched as her fingers touched the wolf's fur, but it proved to be solid and real. The wolf's tongue flicked out, giving Anna's wrist a lick.

"Sue? Is that really you?" Anna whispered, scared to breathe too hard and disrupt the dream.

The wolf whined, rolling its eyes up at the ceiling.

"It must be. Only you would be a smart-ass at a time like this."

The wolf moaned then twitched. Anna backed away, and watched as the wolf changed back into her human friend.

Anna watched in awe. "Sue, you're a werewolf!"

Susan examined her hands. "I can't believe it. I'm not insane." She rubbed her face and ran her fingers through her thick hair. "Werewolves don't seem real."

"Believe me, if I hadn't seen it with my own eyes... even seeing it, I'm starting to doubt my own sanity."

"But it is real!" Susan smiled but then pain shot across her face, "That means I really did kill Jim."

"But why didn't you attack me a minute ago?"

"I don't know!"

"Did you recognize me? Do you remember what happens when you change?"

"Oh I remember, but it's a different kind of memory. Like a dream, but more vivid and easier to recall."

"Are you aware of who you are when you're a wolf?"

"I... I don't know. Right now, here in my room, I knew

you were my friend, but last night was different. I didn't know who Jim was until it was too late. It all happened so fast and I didn't understand what was happening!"

"But it happened again just now! Did you do that on purpose? Can you control when you change?"

"I don't know! I wanted to change. I wanted to show you and I felt really scared that I was losing you in this mess, so maybe I can trigger it somehow, but last night... I had no idea."

"Maybe you can learn to control it?"

"I don't know. I don't think it's that easy. I mean, it's not like I've tried. I've been terrified of doing it again actually, until you got up. I thought you didn't believe me and were going to run away. Suddenly I wanted to change, to show you and I was so scared and that feeling like last night came again and I was able to tap into it... but I'm scared of it Anna. What if I can force it sometimes, but sometimes it goes off on its own? I could be putting everyone in danger. You and Mom and Ben!"

"Calm down." Anna sat on the edge of the bed, reaching out to put a hand on Susan's knee. "You didn't attack me just now, in fact you acted like you! You even answered a question I asked... sort of."

"I did didn't I?" Susan pondered this new turn of events. "It's like, I still see through my own eyes, and I know what's going on, but... it's hard to explain. It's like I'm there in my body, but everything is different."

"Maybe it's something you need to get used to."

"Maybe. But then why did I attack Jim?"

"You tell me. Start from the beginning and don't lie or leave anything out this time."

Anna listened carefully to the whole tale from start to finish. Susan told her about going to see the movie and Jim's idea to hang out afterword. Anna felt awkward when Susan described getting physical with Jim on the ridge, but

Susan spared her no details. Susan faltered when talking about the change, how she didn't feel well and wanted to stop, but Jim didn't understand what was happening. She kept second guessing herself, trying to remember the exact order of events or what something felt like. After the tumble down the hill, the story went on smoothly. Anna guessed that was the part Susan had told many times already.

Anna took a moment to collect her thoughts. "It sounds to me like you were scared."

Susan's lip twitched in disgust, "I was, but that's no reason to attack someone."

"Sometimes when an animal feels cornered and scared, they'll bite even if they normally wouldn't."

"People don't bite."

"Maybe werewolves do. Remember how you said things feel different when you're a wolf? Maybe you have different instincts."

"That's still not an excuse."

"You're looking for a reason to feel bad about this aren't you?"

"And you're looking for a way to get me off the hook!" Susan snapped. She grabbed her pillow mashing it into her face, letting herself scream into it. They sat together in silence for a moment before Susan lowered the pillow again. "Maybe I want to feel bad about this. It's my fault no matter how you look at it."

"It's also an accident no matter how you look at it! It's not like you planned this and you obviously regret it. You have to cut yourself some slack, this whole situation is off the charts bizarre!"

"Maybe you're right, but what do I do about this whole thing? Do I go to the cops and tell them to lock me up? Do I head for the hills and isolate myself so I can't hurt anybody again?"

"Well, for now let's take some time to think about

everything. It's a lot to take in. Give yourself some time to feel bad and to grieve for Jim. This is going to hit everyone hard."

"I can't imagine Jim's family... Oh God, what have I done!" Susan slumped forward.

Anna grabbed Susan's shoulder pulling her up again. "We'll get through this. I promise."

Susan reached over and hugged Anna around the shoulders. "But what if I do it again? What if I'm dangerous?"

"Then put it to the test. Go out into the bush and change. See if you feel like a crazed killer or like you did when you changed in front of me."

"It could be dangerous."

"For the bears maybe."

Susan snorted into Anna's shoulder. "Yeah right. I should try it though. I need to know if I might hurt anyone else."

Anna wanted to reassure Susan and tell her that she wouldn't hurt anyone, but there was no way to be sure, so she held on to Susan's shoulders, hoping she was the one who was right.

CHAPTER 6
FENRIS

The brown 1973 Hornet pulled off the road into an unremarkable motel parking lot. The woman driving stared apprehensively at the greying siding of the motel before cutting the engine. Evee Burns took her time getting out of the car, despite the fact that her younger brother, Les, had already bounded around to her side, anxious to be on their way.

The boy smiled easily as he reached out to pat the hood of the car. "Good thing we made it!"

"You doubted the Hornet?" Evee questioned him.

"Nah, more like the driver!"

Evee shot him her iciest glare.

Les raised his hands in surrender, "Whoa, take it easy sis! I'm just joking around!"

"I know," Evee sighed. This was how Les dealt with stress. He meant well even if his antics were driving her up the wall. Les had a light-hearted nature that balanced out Evee's seriousness, but the siblings were opposites in more than just personality. Les leaned against the car, short and stocky with tanned skin, dark hair and clear First Nations features. He looked nothing like his tall, fair sister with the piercing blue eyes. It amused Evee to watch people struggle to wrap their heads around the idea that they were siblings. The thought lifted her spirits momentarily. "Let's go."

Evee led the way down the row of motel doors before stopping in front of the sixth one. Her heart hammered in her chest. Raising her knuckles she rapped on the door. A flurry of commotion rustled inside before it grew quiet and the door opened. The young man who answered jumped back when he saw her standing at the threshold.

"Ms. Burns! We weren't expecting you until..."

"We drove all night," Evee pushed past him into the room. Pleasantries could wait. That's not why she was here.

Inside, one of the beds had been pushed to the side to make more room around the small table cluttered with papers and computers. The door to the adjoining room hung open and a portly, middle-aged man stormed through it, his face lighting up crimson. His sandy hair was giving way to white and his mustache bristled until his eyes fell on his guests and he smiled. "Evee! It's good to see you again! Come in, come in! It's a blasted mess in here, but we'll fix that for you."

"Don't worry about it Walter. Not on my account." Evee stepped forward meeting Walter with a hearty handshake.

"Well, at least you'll let me introduce you to the team?" Walter gestured at the others gathered in the room, a woman and a man, both dressed in black.

"How many of you are there?" Evee scanned the room, sensing there were more.

"Five, including myself. One team is out at the moment, but we can fill you in." Walter pulled out a chair for her at the cluttered table.

"That's a lot for this type of investigation." Evee felt her hands grow clammy. The room felt too warm and stuffy after being outside.

"Of course it is for a standard case, but you know this

could be more than that!" Walter huffed, puffing out his mustache. "That's why we called you. If we really are up against our old foe again, FENRIS is taking no chances."

The room grew quiet and all eyes fell on Evee. She moved to the chair Walter held out for her, sitting as calmly and casually as she could. "Have you confirmed the sighting?"

"No, not yet. That's why you're here." Walter waited for everyone else to take a seat at the table before grabbing one himself.

"An extra nose or two can't hurt right?" Les leaned back in his chair.

"Quite." Walter folded his hands in front of him on the table. "But noses that know this scent are of particular value to us at this time. We'd like to thank you both for coming."

"You know your thanks is unnecessary. We'd be here regardless." Evee didn't mean to sound harsh, but the longer Walter dallied on formalities, the longer she had to wait for her briefing, which was the only thing standing between her and hunting her prey.

"Yes I know that, and I know how anxious you are to bring this to a resolution, but first things first Evelyn." Walter stared at Evee until she looked away, conceding his leadership. It could have been worse. As regimental as Walter was, when it came down to it, she knew he wanted this as much as she did.

"Right," Walter cleared his throat, "Allow me to introduce you. This fine young lady is Evelyn Burns, and the lad with the cheeky grin plastered across his face is Leslie Burns."

"Please, call me Evee."

"And Les!"

"As you wish." Walter waved at the woman and man in black respectively, "Agents Richards and Park. Now! Let's get down to business! As I mentioned to you on the phone Evee, our little discovery turned out to be a surprise. Richards and Park here were investigating a 242. Standard stuff, but then they had the sighting."

Walter motioned at Park to continue, but he faltered under Evee's gaze, "W... well, uh, ma'am... we're still not one hundred percent sure it's him."

"Which makes sense," Eve said. "We haven't seen hide nor hair from him in over 30 years, and if you've never laid nose to his scent..."

"Agent Park," Walter drew himself up, commanding a presence, "Why don't you start from the beginning?"

"Yes sir. As you said, Richards and I were here investigating a 242 – a potential rogue attack – but immediately we felt it was more like a K19."

"An awakening?" Evee asked, her curiosity piqued.

"Yes ma'am. The victim was a young boy, only 17, his wounds are consistent with those from a large canine. The locals have been cooperative and we've confirmed that it looks like one of us. Anyway, the investigation got shelved when Richards and I went to check out the vic's funeral. It's a small community so half the town was there."

"I can imagine the death of someone so young would be felt strongly in a little place like this." Evee's heart went out to them.

"Absolutely! We were checking out people close to the boy for possible leads when I spotted him. I was surprised because we don't have one of *them* registered for this area."

"Watch your tone Park," Walter grumbled a warning.

"Begging your pardon sir. I wouldn't normally... but the way he smelled! You know how sometimes *they* smell off, but this one was rank! He fit the Hunter's description, scent and all. He clearly wasn't human and wasn't supposed to be in this area. Plus given his proximity to the vic..."

"Did he see you?" Evee asked the question plaguing her mind.

"I can't be sure. We were downwind and he didn't acknowledge us."

"None the less," Walter said, "We are treating this as if he knows we are here."

"But wouldn't he have run by now if he knew we were here?" Richards spoke up.

"No. He'd only step up his timeline." A chill spread through Evee's blood. "He'd be on his guard after the K19 anyway. He knows our patterns."

"You don't think he's responsible for the boy?" Park asked.

"Not this again." Walter rolled his eyes. "You confirmed yourself it had to be one of us!"

"Yes but Hunter's really old isn't he? We don't know the extent of his abilities!"

"Some of us know more than we'd like." Evee fought back the flood of memories that would only keep her from the task at hand. "Besides, it doesn't matter. The boy is dead and Hunter's going to use his death to draw us in. We're compromised before we even start. We need confirmation he's here. If he is we're wasting daylight."

"That may be, but you're not going to go running off without the final piece of the puzzle." Walter flipped through a pile of papers on the table before extracting a photo.

"What do you mean?"

"There may or may not be a connection, but if we're right about this being an awakening, it might be worth following up on. The victim was out in the woods when he was attacked. This is the girl who was with him." Walter slid the labelled photo across the table.

Evee picked up the photo, scanning over an unremarkable teenage girl. She didn't get Walter's joke until she read the name on the label and laughed out loud.

"What is it?" Les asked.

"Her last name is Wolfe!" Evee slammed the photo back on the table.

"Despite that fact, I don't think she's aware of her heritage," Walter said.

Evee felt the pit of her stomach drop. Before she knew it she was on her feet heading for the door, the photo of the girl in hand.

Walter jumped up to cut her off. "And where do you think you're going?"

"Walter don't you see, this is the perfect storm!" Evee waved the photo desperately in his face.

Walter held up a hand, forcing Evee to stop. "Explain."

"This!" Evee held the photo between them. "This is our connection! Right here! He knows, Walter! He's probably known since he arrived in this town that this girl is one of us but she didn't know it! He's been waiting for this! For her to awaken and us to come running!"

Walter grew grave as the situation sunk in. "Do you think the girl will be his next victim?"

"Argh!" Evee paced around the room, her mind running in circles. "It could be her if he really wants to mess with our heads, but I don't think so. It's not his style, she's too obvious, too strong. No, if you ask me it'll be someone close to her though. This girl and everyone she cares about are in danger. Make no mistake though," Evee froze staring at Walter, "He's been planning this one for a long time."

"Which means we can't be too careful." Walter placed a firm hand on Evee's shoulder. "An awakening complicates things..."

"He knows it will! He's counting on that! Walter we don't have time to do this by-the-book!"

"Says who?" Les jumped up from the table. "I can offer to be the girl's advocate, I'm already registered with FENRIS."

Walter ran his fingers through his hair tugging at the strands. "She's not even going to know what that is Les! Even if she agrees, it's stretching protocol!"

"One child is dead already Walter." Evee stressed the urgency of the situation. "We have a chance to save the next."

"You're right Evee, someone's life is on the line, and I'm not going to let anyone screw this up because they didn't think things through first!"

"Please!" Les pushed his way between Walter and Evee. "There's no reason we can't do this properly and quickly. Send Evee and me out to meet the girl and assess the situation. I know what I'm doing. I won't push it if it looks dangerous, for the girl or anyone else. You both have to trust me on this one."

Walter gritted his teeth, holding in a snarl, but took a step back rubbing the tension out of his face with a calloused palm. "Alright. I will put my trust in you Les, if you promise to keep your sister in line! I trust your judgment. You have my leave to make contact with the girl, but only if you think it's safe to do so and won't compromise the case."

"I won't let you down sir!" Les bounced forward grabbing his sister's arm, leading her to the door.

"Yes, both of you get out of my sight before I change my mind!" Walter growled.

Evee needed no further bidding, leaving the FENRIS agents to their business.

They were halfway to the car when Les nudged her with his elbow. "Aren't you glad you brought me along?"

Evee wanted to smack the smug smile right off her brother's face. "Thrilled. Now get your tail in the car before I bite it off!"

CHAPTER 7
TEST RUN

Something was wrong, something deep in the pit of Susan's stomach. Hands closed around her, iron bars forming a cage. She strained against them, but struggling only made them tighter. Her emotions – normally wrapped up so neatly – began to unravel. Fear howled through her and anger frothed at the mouth, threatening to overrun her body. She tried to control them, but it was like holding sand, the harder she squeezed, the more escaped. Clouds rolled away from the darkness revealing a piercingly bright moon, exerting its pull over her raging emotions. Susan fought for control, but her body wouldn't respond. Then the world turned red, the moon reflecting a ghastly crimson and suddenly Susan could move again. However, her hands and feet felt like they were sticking to the ground beneath her. Susan looked down and Jim's terrified, dead face stared back at her. Susan cried out, but all that came out was a howl.

Throwing her covers in every direction, Susan bolted upright. Her skin went cold as the sweat drenching her pajamas met the air of her bedroom. She raised a hand to wipe her face, but couldn't stop her fingers trembling, so she shoved them back under the sheets. Her chest heaved, and she focused on taking deep breaths. Eventually her hammering heart slowed, and her muscles released.

Another nightmare. It had been the same every night since the accident. Since she killed Jim. Fresh guilt flooded Susan and she drew her knees to her chest, squeezing herself into a ball. Every morning was the same. She woke up terrified only to be reminded that she was the most terrifying thing in the room.

Susan released her knees, throwing her legs over the side of the bed and springing to her feet. She needed to do something. She needed to escape the endless wheel of torment her mind kept reciting for her. She needed to go for a run.

Susan hadn't been out for a run since that night, which was strange because this was the time she could have used a run the most. Everything in the past week had been a blur of mourning, police, doctors, news broadcasts, tears and grieving.

School had been a bad idea. Susan thought she could escape if she buried herself in work, but then the looks in the halls and the half audible whispers that she had "found Jim" were more than she could take. Susan was unprepared for the amount of sympathy people gave her. She didn't want it. She didn't deserve it. It was enough to make her want to scream at everyone, but that rage was quickly doused by the fear of what might happen if she lashed out at anyone. So Susan had been reigning everything in, keeping a tight lid on her emotions.

The funeral was by far the most trying. Seeing Jim's grieving family, Susan wanted to throw herself at their feet and beg for forgiveness. It was evident that the small community had been shaken by Jim's death as the turn out for the funeral was astronomical. Susan bore witness to it all. It was the least she could do. It was the only thing she could do, but it didn't ease her suffering. Then again, she wanted to suffer. She deserved it. After all, it was her fault.

Susan pulled some running clothes out from the piles of dirty laundry littering her bedroom floor. She dressed herself mechanically then snuck down the hall toward the back door as quietly as possible. It was still early and her mother and brother were sleeping. She didn't want to wake them. She also didn't want to have an argument with her mother about how going into the bush this time of year was dangerous because the bears were hungry and preparing to hibernate. Susan stifled a laugh. She was probably more dangerous than any old black bear. She ran her fingers over her running shoes as she put them on, tugging the laces into place. She stood at the back entrance for a moment, but the house remained quiet. Satisfied she hadn't disturbed anyone, Susan reached for the door.

The outside world was grey. Clouds diffused the morning light of the November sky, threatening rain, or possibly snow. The bush was quiet save for the wind rippling through barren branches. It was early in the morning, but the hazy light made it hard to tell the exact time. Everything smelled old and brittle, waiting for winter to spread its frozen shroud over it.

Susan waded through the limp grass of the lawn, heading for the mouth of a trail that lead down toward the creek. Her breath misted before her and the cold air stung her throat. The bush held a damp tang to it, full of wet leaves and wood, along with mushrooms past their prime. Rotting vegetation was making its winter bed, settling in for the long nights and short days ahead.

Susan broke into a run when she hit the trail, shaking the chill from her legs. At first her muscles protested, but the punishing ache satisfied her. She pushed on, finding her stride. It was easy going, since the trail started with a steep hill winding its way down to the creek. Gravity pulled her down, but Susan relished the feeling of control as she descended at a steady pace. After a week of living in fear of her own body, running was reassuring.

The trail opened up and wove alongside the creek. Susan stamped her feet into the earth, picking up speed, letting herself go. She should have gone out earlier, but denying herself the pleasure of freedom seemed appropriate at the time. She didn't deserve to feel good about anything, but maybe running would keep her in check. Susan ran faster, pushing herself up a hill towards an outcrop of rock. She dug in, fighting gravity as hard as she could. Then the hill crested and the resistance melted away.

Susan came to a stop and let her breathing go ragged. Her legs trembled underneath her as she leaned forward, the cold air tearing at her throat. A metallic tang stirred in her mouth but she spat it out. She had pushed too hard, but that was fine. Standing upright Susan took in the view from the top of the hill. The grey light from the clouds made everything look bleak and dead, but without leaves in the way she could see far over the hills. It was strangely quiet and desolate in the bush, as if every living thing was hiding from her.

"Perfect," The wind snatched the word from her mouth and silence permeated her world again. She was alone in the middle of nowhere, where she couldn't hurt another living thing even if she tried. Susan had banished all thought of trying to change into a wolf on purpose. The thought of losing control and hurting someone else was too terrifying to entertain. But out here, in this bleak stand of trees and rocks, there wasn't anyone to hurt except herself.

A tall oak tree rose above the crown of the hill, its branches of brown, withered leaves sweeping up over the rocks. Susan scampered down a small stoney shelf, towards its bole. There was a little shelter from the wind between the rocks and the tree. Susan stripped off her hoodie, and continued peeling off layers of clothes, trying not to think about the cold air biting at her skin. Stuffing her clothes in the crook of a branch, Susan crouched down curling herself into a ball to keep warm. It struck her as ridiculous, crouching naked in the woods this time of year, but it couldn't be helped. She needed to be as far away from people as possible and she didn't want to get tangled in her stupid clothes again. At least her body was still warm from her run, but her sweat stung as it cooled on her skin.

Susan clenched her teeth together to keep them from chattering and closed her eyes trying to remember how she had changed before. She willed her body to change, but nothing happened. It was somewhat a relief to know it wasn't that easy. If she could figure out how to trigger the change maybe she could control it. Susan searched for an answer. The other times she wolfed out, there had been a sense of urgency, almost desperation, but right now, there was only the cold making her uncomfortable. There had to be something to it, like an emotional connection, or maybe it was spiritual. She couldn't put her finger on it.

A chill spread through Susan's body. She fought to subdue the shivers it induced. She needed to focus. Thinking about changing wasn't going to make it happen. She had to connect with something more primal than her thoughts. It was a dangerous place to go, but Susan opened the vault of emotions she had locked away to keep herself in check through the horrid week she'd gone through. Grief pricked tears in her eyes and a hole of guilt grew in her chest. She gave in and let herself cry and her body shake. The release felt good, but it also brought with it a familiar feeling – the growl – hiding this time in the back of her throat. Susan tried to grab onto it, but whenever she tried it would slip away. Maybe it couldn't be corralled after all. Or maybe she couldn't force it, only open up and let it take over.

Susan took a deep breath and relaxed as much as she could. She was terrified, but she had to try. As she opened up to the growl, a tingling sensation rewarded her, followed by a familiar twitching of her skin. Changing was uncomfortable, but the less she fought it, the quicker and easier it happened.

Susan no longer felt cold. There was a new barrier between her and the wind. The temperature felt almost balmy and Susan couldn't imagine why anyone would need clothes in this weather. Looking down at her feet Susan saw she was covered in white and tawny fur the same colour as her hair.

She lifted her hand, watching as the paw rose in kind. She seemed to be in control. Susan sat on her haunches, taking her time to feel the new arrangement of her muscles, slowly stretching and flexing her body. She rose to her feet, shifting her weight, feeling her new balance on all fours. As odd as it felt, her legs were sturdy enough beneath her.

After taking stock of herself, Susan turned her attention to the bush around her. It had changed too. The forest was alive with smells and sounds she had only a vague sense of before, but the colours were muted and dull, as if something was missing. The browns of the forest weren't the same and everything looked grey and green instead, as if she was looking through a tinted lens.

Susan's ears swiveled as they caught a rustling in the leaves. She followed the sound, surprised to find the squirrel that had caused it was much farther away than she expected. Her perception was off and would take some getting used to. All in all though, she didn't feel horribly wild or out of control like she had before. Susan felt like herself, even if it was a distorted version. She was aware of who she was. That was a start.

Susan picked up her feet and tried moving forward. It seemed easy enough. One paw after another. She sprang forward breaking into a run, but fell into a tangle of legs crashing though the leaves. Susan righted herself and shook her coat free of debris. Shaking was an odd sensation, and it happened without her thinking about it. It was pure instinct. Maybe that was the difference between her human self and her wolf self. Humans think too much. Perhaps this side of her wasn't meant to be controlled. It was instinct, pure and unfettered. The wolf simply was. It did what was needed in the moment. Guilt trickled down the back of her mind. Listening to your instincts was all well and good, but in the end, without a conscience, it could make you a monster.

Susan pawed the earth. It smelled rich and welcoming. She lay down in the loam and rolled onto her back, enjoying the smell. She got to her feet again, but froze as a new scent penetrated the air. Someone was coming. No wait, not one but two new scents were emerging. Susan shivered. She didn't know how she knew, but these two weren't human. She crouched down, ready to defend herself. Running wasn't an option. She could hear them now, approaching from the trail she had come down.

The first visitor approached head on without hesitation. Something about it was familiar, and Susan realized it was because it smelled like her as a wolf. Susan drew back her lips, growling a warning. Sure enough, a wolf crested the hill, but it was unlike any wolf Susan had ever seen. It was soft white with the most unsettling blue eyes – eyes no natural wolf would have. It peered down at Susan, unconcerned. Susan was unsure what to make of this creature. It had a lovely warm scent, but before Susan could finish evaluating the white wolf, the second animal appeared. It was smaller and much more unassuming than the wolf. In fact it was a coyote. His smell was more natural, like the wind and grass. Despite herself, Susan relaxed, at ease with the second interloper. Her growl quieted, though she remained crouched, ready for anything.

The coyote pranced forward, sniffing at the tree where Susan had stashed her clothes, then carefully approached Susan herself. He circled her slowly, studying her through hazel eyes, then he winked at her and his body began to change.

Susan jumped back. The change was disconcerting to watch and she wondered if that was what she looked like when it happened to her. Instead of becoming fully human however, the coyote turned into something in between. He grew larger, his limbs elongated and muzzle shortened, but fur still covered his body. He flashed what Susan interpreted as a smile and then he did something that shocked her. He spoke.

"Susan Wolfe I presume?"

We can talk? Susan tried to say, but all that came out of her mouth were garbled sounds.

"I'll take that as a yes." The coyote-boy flashed his teeth at her.

The white wolf approached and also semi-shifted into a half-human half-wolf. "Are you alright Susan? Can you shift out?" Its voice was low, but unmistakably feminine.

Susan didn't understand what she was being asked. The words rattled around in her brain not making sense.

"She means can you change back into a human on your own?" The coyote interpreted.

Susan eyed the boy sideways and nodded.

"Don't be afraid, we won't hurt you." The coyote's face was too soft and friendly not to believe.

Susan's chest burned as if it was splitting in two. Finally, there was someone who would understand, maybe even hold her accountable for what she had done. She wanted to cry, but all that came out was a hiccup and a whimper.

"It's alright." The coyote reached out a hand to reassure her. As his fingers touched her shoulder, Susan's skin flinched, but she allowed his hand to settle. If he had meant her harm, he and the white wolf could have ripped her apart by now.

The coyote pointed at himself. "Can you turn into a true

werewolf yet, like this?"

Susan shook her head. She didn't even know that was possible.

"OK, then how about you shift back into a human and we'll have a little chat?"

"And don't even think about running away," The wolf growled. "I guarantee, I'm faster than you."

"Evee!" The coyote scolded her, "Can't you smell she's scared?"

"Obviously. That's why I warned her. In case she gets any bright ideas."

"Ignore her," The coyote waved the wolf away. "That's what I do anyway."

The white wolf stormed off, grumbling to herself, while the boy followed Susan over to the oak tree. Susan wondered if he was going to watch her change back, but before she could try, the boy was on the other side of the tree, facing away. Susan willed herself to change and this time it came without a fuss. The cold air bit into her exposed skin once more, and Susan scrambled to get dressed. When she was finished she peeked around the tree, but the coyote was gone. A bark drew Susan's attention to a little hollow halfway down the hill where the wolf and coyote were sitting, sheltered from the wind.

The thought of running did occur to Susan, but she had no doubt the wolf would make good on its threat, so she walked over to the hollow where she had been summoned.

"Who are you?" Susan studied their faces, still unsure what they wanted from her.

"My name is Leslie Burns," the coyote said, "And this is my sister, Evelyn. But you can call us Les and Evee."

Something about the word 'sister' didn't click. "You're related?"

Evee laughed, "Like clockwork! Don't worry, you're not the first, nor will you be the last to second guess us."

"Well, technically we're only pack siblings," Les corrected

her, "But that's kind of a long story. Unfortunately we don't have time for that right now. We're here to talk about you Susan."

The pit of Susan's stomach dropped. "You're here about Jim aren't you?"

Les' eyes softened, "Yes, we are, but that's not the only reason we're here. Let me start out by saying that we're here to help you, despite this big grump sitting next to me."

"Call me Sue." Despite wanting to be cautious, Susan also wanted someone she could trust with her secret. Les seemed like he would listen.

"Right, Sue then," Les said, "We're here as representatives of a world you now find yourself neck deep in. Clearly you are aware that you are a werewolf..."

Werewolf. Susan let the word sink in. It was official. Then her mind reeled, "Wait, what do you mean, 'world'? How many of us are there?"

"Many." Evee glared at her.

"I know you probably have lots of questions Sue," Les said. "It's going to be a lot to take in for the first little while. Basically we're a community within the wider human world. We're nowhere near as numerous as humans but we live among them all over the world."

"How come I've never heard of you then?"

"Well, we try to stay under the radar, so to speak. Like a shadow to the human world, always there out of the corner of your eye, but whenever you look straight at us, you miss us."

"This is insane." Susan plunked herself on a rock near the edge of the hollow, trying to register this information.

"Any more insane than turning into a wolf?" Les laughed. "Look, I know it's a lot to take in but we're here to help."

"How?" Susan spat out the word as if it left a bitter taste in her mouth. "Jim's dead. There's nothing you can do to fix that."

"No. We can't change things for Jim, but we can help you."

"What makes you think I want your help?"

Les spoke slowly, "We're here for you Sue, to guide you through the ins and outs of our world and the pending investigation on the death of James Schenn."

It was too much. If these strangers wanted her head they might as well take it now. "Well I did it! I'm the one who killed him, so case closed! We can all go home now!"

"It's not that simple Sue." Les' face took on a pained expression.

"It's not?" Susan's voice rose. "What's so difficult for you to understand? I'm a monster! I killed someone!"

"And you clearly feel remorse about it!" Les reasoned with her. "Being a werewolf can be anything but simple when you have no idea how to control the power you have at your disposal."

"Tell that to Jim's family!" Susan mustered as much venom as she could, no longer bothering to contain her rage.

"I know you feel responsible Sue, but it's not your fault." Les' kindness was scathing.

"Then who's fault is it?! Who do I get to blame?!" Susan yelled, but the faces before her remained motionless and hard to read. Tears blurred her vision so she shoved her face into her knees and began to sob.

A hand stroked Susan's shoulder and she looked up surprised to see the white wolf sheltering her, her blue eyes flooded with concern. "Sue, I'm so sorry you've gone through this. Losing someone you care about is a terrible thing to go through and it's even worse when you feel you're the one responsible."

Susan fell into Evee's arms and cried. Her fur was surprisingly soft and her presence comforting. Letting her anger and grief go lifted a heavy weight off Susan's chest, but the empty hole in its place made her feel like she was learning to breath all over again.

"There now," Evee stroked Susan's back. "I know this is hard for you, and normally we wouldn't be pushing you like this, but Jim's death isn't the only reason we're here."

"Evee," Les warned, "I don't think we should be putting extra stress on Susan right now."

"What do you mean?" Susan sat up. "What else is going on?"

"Look," Les shook his head, clearly weighing how much to say and how much to hold back, "We've got a lot to go over in a short period of time and we're already putting you through the ringer."

"No, it's fine." Susan rubbed the tears away with her palms, straightening her back, trying to appear as put together as she could. "I'm fine. I'm sorry I yelled at you guys."

"It's to be expected." Evee pulled away, watching Susan carefully.

"So what do we do now?" Susan wiped her tear stained face with her sleeve.

"Well, we still have a lot of things to explain to you, and when we're done, if you want I can be the one to represent you in our system," Les said.

"What? Like a lawyer or something?"

"Something like that. We're called advocates, and since you're a minor with no known werewolf relatives, you need an elder to represent and guide you."

"An 'elder'?" Susan snorted. At least Les was making her laugh. "Come on, you can't be that much older than me!"

"I'm older than I look." Les grinned, challenging Susan to question him further.

Susan didn't want any more confrontation so she looked up at the sky, "I should be getting home, my Mom will freak out if she wakes up and I'm not around. Wait, what about my Mom? Should I tell her about this?"

"Normally, we'd be contacting your parents right away, but due to extenuating circumstances..." Les scratched his head, leaving his words hang.

Susan's head began to throb. "Fine. I won't say anything right now, but at least let me go home and come up with some excuse to leave the house. Then we can meet someplace and you can tell me everything I need to know."

CHAPTER 8
A TRUTH AND A LIE

The house remained quiet when Susan slipped in through the back door. Tossing her sneakers aside, she padded down the hall toward the bathroom. Normally, she would set the shower a little cooler after a run, but after the conversation on the hill and the walk home, a chill had spread through her limbs. Steam flooded out from the shower as Susan jumped in, rubbing her arms under the hot water, trying to rub out the chill. As she warmed herself in the cascading water, her mind busily unravelled and put back together everything that happened outside.

She was a werewolf. That much was certain. Whether or not she was a danger to others remained up for debate, but it would seem she did have some degree of control over her powers. There were others like her too. Whatever their motives, they existed. She wasn't alone. They may or may not have answers for her, but it was as good a place as any to start. The only way to find out would be to meet them later. She needed to talk to them.

The clanking of dishes echoed from the kitchen as Susan stepped into the hall. Her mother was finally awake and from the smell of things, making breakfast. Susan's stomach grumbled as she quickly rummaged through her clothes, trying to find something clean to wear.

Susan entered the kitchen, calm and clean, taking a seat at the counter, ready for breakfast. Eggs sizzled in the pan and Susan enjoyed a moment of near silence before the onslaught began.

"You were up early." Her mother didn't miss a beat. "Did you go out for a run?"

"Um yeah..." Susan's mind spun. So far so normal.

"Did you go up the road? I hope you weren't out back this time of year."

"No, I stayed on the road." Susan lied, ignoring the guilt tugging at her conscience.

"Isn't it getting too cold out for running?"

"I warm up once I get going. It's only hard when the snow starts and everything gets slushy."

"Which might be sooner than later with the weather we've been having. And it was so nice out a week ago!"

"Mmm hmm," Susan acknowledged her mother, but began to zone out from the conversation, calculating the amount of time she'd need to drive across town to meet Les and Evee.

"Sue?" Her mother interrupted her thoughts. "Toast?"

"Oh, yeah, sure. Hey Mom can I borrow the car today, I need to go downtown."

"What for?"

"Just... shopping." Susan maintained her composure, but could feel her palms getting clammy. White lies and banter were one thing, but this felt different.

"Oh are you going to the Superstore? Could you pick up a few things while you're there?"

"No Mom, I'm going with Anna. We're just going to hang out for a bit."

"Alright then." Susan's mom began dishing out the eggs

as if nothing out of the ordinary was happening.

Susan relaxed. Finally her Mom was cutting her some slack. Not wanting to waste this opportunity, Susan shoveled down her food, making as hasty an exit as possible.

"You could at least chew your food instead of wolfing it down!" Susan's mom scolded.

Susan choked. Something went down the wrong way and she coughed.

"See what I mean?"

Susan gulped down water, instead of trying to find an excuse. Her mom could have this victory. "Sorry, I was really hungry after my run. I'll chew next time. Gotta go!"

Susan drove out to the Tim Horton's at the south end of Timber Creek where she was supposed to meet the Burns siblings. She sat for a moment after parking the car, trying to unravel her thoughts again, but it was no use. There was only one thing to do. She stepped out of the car, but stopped when she saw the people milling through the windows of the coffee shop. She wasn't sure who she was looking for as she had no idea what the Burns' looked like as humans. Susan laughed at the thought of a werewolf lining up for its morning coffee.

A familiar scent hit Susan's nose and she turned to see a boy waving at her from a bench across the parking lot. It had to be Les. The resemblance was obvious, down to the smug grin and the twinkle in his eye. Sitting next to him was an older woman, probably in her thirties, who appeared to be ignoring Susan, focusing instead on a the steaming cup of tea in her hand. Susan made her way across the parking lot and when she got close, Les jumped up to meet her.

"Did you want to get something?" Les tilted his cup towards the coffee shop. "My treat!"

"Uh, no thanks, I'm fine. I'm not much of a coffee drinker." Susan was anxious to get on with their conversation.

"Suit yourself." Les took a sip from his cup.

"Let's take a walk." Evee rose from the bench, pushing back a lock of brown hair, before eying Susan.

Susan felt Evee's cold stare boring into her and she looked away. Suddenly Susan felt lighter as if there had been tension in the air that she hadn't noticed. She followed Evee and Les strolled along beside her. Together they meandered down the streets of the nearby suburb. Susan's mind raced with questions, but she wasn't sure where to start.

Les took the conversation past pleasantries, "So I take it your family doesn't know then? About the wolf stuff?"

"No. They don't." Susan hadn't had anyone to talk to about her struggles besides Anna, and even then, there was no way Anna could understand.

"I see." Les chewed at the rim of his now empty coffee cup. "Is there anyone who does?"

Susan's heart jumped into her throat. "What happens if someone does know? Or even if they find out by accident?"

"Don't worry." Les reassured her. "It's not the end of the world if someone finds out, or suspects. We'll deal with it. Normally we encourage getting family involved, especially seeing as how they may share the bloodline."

"Bloodline? So it's hereditary?"

"Bingo! No bites or transfer of bodily fluids required, it's all in your genetics!"

"So this could happen to my Mom or my brother?" Susan shuddered. She didn't wish what she'd gone through on anyone, least of all her family.

"It's unlikely to affect your mother." Evee dropped back to walk by Susan's other side. "Awakenings seldom happen past middle age, but she may be a carrier."

"Most people awaken around puberty." Les bumped her arm playfully with his elbow. "Gives new meaning to *the change* doesn't it?"

Susan laughed, her tight chest making it sound sharp. "Because going through puberty isn't fun enough already... but wait, if it's hereditary, shouldn't you have an idea who's a werewolf and who isn't? How come no one warned me?"

"The answer is that we don't know." Evee stared off into the distance. "Many bloodlines have been lost to us over the years. We haven't always been this organized."

"But you're organized now?" Susan said. "And you have your own system and rules and everything?"

"We try to operate under the laws of our human hosts for the most part," Les said. "But then there are certain things that humans don't have laws to govern, or we feel they don't apply to us. That's where we come in."

"Right," Susan drew out the word. "Where did you say you came from again?"

"The bureau that governs all werewolf comings and goings is called FENRIS." Les threw her a cheeky grin. "You'll become very intimate with their workings over the next little while..."

"Because of Jim?"

"Yes," Les opened his mouth to say more, but instead scratched the back of his head and looked to Evee.

Evee's face was grim, "There's also a complication."

"That you keep mentioning but haven't told me anything about!" Susan stomped her foot on the pavement drawing their walk to a halt.

"We have a situation," Evee's voice remained level and calm, "One that is not your fault, but may be connected to you and your awakening. Your case is actually the lower priority right now."

Susan's skin went cold, "What could be more important than a murder investigation?"

Evee caught Susan square in her gaze, "Preventing another death."

Susan froze, unable to form words to express her shock.

Evee continued, "Susan, I'm very sorry for what you've

gone through and everything you're about to go through, but we have reason to believe a dangerous criminal is here in Timber Creek…"

"Whoa, like what kind of criminal? A werewolf? I thought we could control ourselves?"

"Control is learned," Les said. "Some have an easier time with it than others. In the end though, we have as much free will as any human, and like humans you get some bad apples."

"This criminal is one of us," Evee said, "And we deal with our own kind in cases like this. He's killed before and he'll kill again. It's only a matter of time."

Susan took a moment to stare at her feet as everything swirled through her head. "What can I do to help?"

Les put a hand firmly on Susan's shoulder, "You're already helping by cooperating with us. I know this is hard for you, and I promise we'll deal with your case as soon as we deal with our little friend first."

"We call him Hunter," Evee's lips tightened at the name, "But he could be operating under any alias, disguising himself as human. We've been chasing him for many years, but he's cunning. What's worse is that he enjoys taunting us. It's all a game in his twisted little mind."

"Sounds like a real nice guy," Susan said.

"Actually," Evee said, "He can be quite charming when he wants to be. He blends in with humans extremely well. He's done it for years, and he's good at what he does."

"And you think this killer – this Hunter – might be connected to me somehow?"

"Not so much connected as close to you," Les said. "You were not aware of what you were or that there were others like you, but he's probably known about you right from the start."

Susan wracked her brain. She couldn't picture anyone she knew being a cold blooded serial killer, but then, maybe it was someone she didn't know all that well. "So what's this

Hunter guy like? You said you've been after him for years. How old is he?"

"That's not so easy to answer," Les hinted at something as if he wanted Susan to guess.

Susan took the bait, "Why?"

"We age differently from humans," Evee said. "We can live for a long time, and often we pause at certain stages in our development. No one really knows why, but there's a chance Hunter's just as young as he used to be or that he's aged significantly."

"How long is a long time?" Susan couldn't tell if Les was joking, but Evee seemed genuinely serious. "Do we live forever?"

"No," Les laughed, "But a few hundred years is not too shabby."

"Are you serious?"

Les pointed proudly to his chest, "I'm over a hundred, give or take a decade."

"That's not even funny."

"I know! You think you have problems, I've been a teenager for over a hundred years!"

Susan was about to laugh at the absurdity of it all when her phone buzzed in her coat pocket. Her stomach lurched as her home number flashed on the screen. "I need to take this guys. One sec."

The phone was barely to her ear when her mother's voice burst from it. "Susan where are you!?"

"I told you Mom, I'm out shopping..."

"With Anna right?"

Guilt welled in Susan's stomach, "Yeah, like I said this morning."

"Then would you care to explain to me why Anna answered the phone when I called the Russel's?"

Panic spread up Susan's throat like wildfire. "I uh... I just wanted to get out of the house OK."

"No it's not OK. Where are you?"

"I'm fine, I'm down at the Tim's in the south end. I'm out for a walk with some friends."

"Susan Wolfe, you get in my car and drive your sorry butt home right now. We'll talk about this when you get home."

Susan hung up the phone, holding it at arms length, staring blankly at the screen.

Les broke the silence, "That didn't sound good."

"It's not. I kind of lied to my Mom about where I was and now she's freaking out."

"You lied to your Mom?" Les grimaced as if he had stepped on something sharp.

"What was I supposed to tell her? Bye Mom, I'm meeting up with a couple of strangers I met this morning. By the way they're werewolves, but don't worry, they haven't bitten my head off yet!"

"I get it," Les said. "We've put you in a tight spot, so let's take a minute and think about what we're going to do next."

"There is no we!" Susan said, irritated. "I'm going home. I lied to my Mom and now she's freaking out. I'm probably going to be grounded for the rest of my life, so I don't know what you think I'm going to be able to do to help you."

"I understand." Les's calm, level tone was more grating than reassuring. "I'm sorry Sue, we've screwed things up."

"No, I got myself into this, I'll get myself out… just give me some time to go home and talk to my Mom."

"Maybe we should go with you." Evee stepped forward.

"Evee, you know we can't right now." Les stood in front of her, blocking her way.

"Why the Hell, not? We've already made contact, and things are only going to get more complicated! Screw protocol!"

"FENRIS will have our tails…"

"Look!" Susan held up her hands stepping between the siblings. "I'll sort this out OK. Just give me some time."

"We might not have time." Evee's normally level voice wavered.

Les pushed his sister back, handing Susan a card. "We'll give you an hour. If you can't sort it out on your own, we're going to have to step in. Call me when you've sorted things out with your Mom, or if you change your mind and want our help."

Susan took the card, running her fingers over the embossed letters and numbers. "Thanks Les. I'll call soon, I promise."

She hadn't even made it back to the car before Anna called in a panic, asking frantically if Susan was alright. She had really done it this time. Not only was her Mom mad at her, but now Anna was freaking out as well. They both panicked over the smallest things. It was amazing how one little white lie was turning into a disaster. She would be pushing her Mom's patience and her hour ultimatum, but Susan needed to stop at Anna's on the way home to do some damage control.

Anna was already waiting for her on the curb outside of her house. Clouds loomed overhead making everything grey. Susan pulled over to the side of the road. She hadn't even gotten out of the car before Anna was in her face.

"Are you crazy? You're mom's going to kill you!" Anna's normally pale skin was drained of colour, looking like paper in the grey light.

"Tell me something I don't know!" Susan slammed the Honda door.

"You could have told me, I would have covered for you."

"I didn't think about it. I'm sorry!" Susan's hands flew into the air.

"What's so important you couldn't tell me?" Hurt replaced Anna's frustration.

"No, it's not like that... I didn't..." Susan's world was swimming. She pressed her fingers to her temples and focused. "I didn't think things through because I was in a rush. I couldn't tell my mom. Jesus, I just wanted her off my back for five minutes!"

"But you drag me into this?"

"I didn't think she would find out! I was only supposed to be gone for a couple of hours..."

"Doing what?! What is so important you couldn't at least give me a heads up?"

Susan stared at Anna, taking in a sharp breath. "There are others like me. Other werewolves. They found me this morning on a run, but Mom doesn't know anything about the wolf stuff, and I can't tell her right now. I don't even know what's going on, and suddenly someone's there offering me a lifeline. I had to take it."

"And you didn't think to tell anyone where you were going? What if they did something to you Sue?"

"They're not like that..."

"Oh I suppose you're real good friends after meeting for five minutes."

"You wouldn't understand."

Something snapped behind Anna's eyes. "Right. I wouldn't understand what it's like to be different, to have a secret you can't tell anybody. How could I possibly know what it's like to have people assume you're normal on the outside, but on the inside you're struggling to keep this screaming urge in check."

Susan opened her mouth to protest, but something in Anna's voice stopped her. There was something there. Something Susan couldn't remember.

Anna let the full force of her fury out, "How could I understand? How could *you* understand?! You've been a werewolf for a week and you're falling apart! Now imagine keeping that secret with no one to talk to! Try lying to everyone, even your best friend because you're terrified you'd lose them if they knew the truth."

Realization crawled up Susan's spine, "Anna, I..."

"No! Shut up! Just shut up and listen for once. It's always about you Sue! You said you'd make time and you never did. But then what could possibly compare to being a werewolf? It must be so hard. Not like being gay! That's so yesterday! Kids are over it these days, especially in small towns."

The pieces clicked into place. Susan had been so wrapped up in her own problems that she completely forgot about that nagging little puzzle she was trying to coax out of Anna. Now it was all laid out in front of her. "I... I'm sorry Anna."

"Forget it!"

"No wait! I know I've been wrapped up in this whole thing, and..."

"You don't get it do you Sue?! You don't need me anymore. You have new friends who can clearly help you more than I ever could. Go play fetch with them and leave me alone!"

"No! Anna!" Susan reached forward to grab her arm, but Anna pulled away at the touch.

"Leave me alone!" Anna screamed and turned to run down the street.

Susan wanted to follow but her legs rooted themselves to the ground. She had never seen Anna so angry. She didn't know what to do. She wanted to fix it, to make everything alright, but she knew Anna wouldn't hear it right now. Anna needed to blow off some steam, and Susan needed to let her. She shuffled her way back to the car when her phone rang again. It was her mom. Susan leaned against the car as she lifted the phone to her ear.

"Where are you?" Her mother's worried voice echoed through the phone.

"Apologizing to Anna." Susan thumped her head against the car.

"I thought you were coming straight home?"

"Yeah well seeing as how you'll probably lock me up and throw away the key when I get there, I figured I might want to apologize to my best friend for throwing her under the bus!"

A deep sigh came from the phone. "And how is that going?"

"She's pissed! She won't even talk to me!"

"Sue, I don't know what's going on. I know you're having a hard time right now, but I'm here for you. Come home and we'll talk about it. I promise I won't throw away the key."

Tears welled in Susan's eyes. "But you might lock me up?"

"We'll see about that."

Her mom was being reasonable. After all, she had no idea what was really going on. Maybe it was time to tell her the truth. Susan agreed to come home, but no sooner had she hung up then she was reaching into her coat pocket, fumbling with a little paper card and mashing numbers into her phone.

"Hello?" A cheery voice answered.

"Hey Les, it's Sue."

"Oh hey! How's it going with your Mom?"

"I haven't even made it home yet."

"Really, you live that far?"

"No, I stopped at Anna's – my best friend's – to apologize for getting her in trouble. But then we got into a huge fight, and she ran off. She's so mad at me! This is all my fault!"

"It'll be fine Sue. I'm sure she'll come to understand."

"That's just it though! She's the only person who understands..." Susan bit her lip before rushing into her confession, "Les, I told her about everything! I've even changed in front of her! And now she's so mad at me she actually ran off."

"Whoa, wait a sec, she knows you're a werewolf?"

"Yeah..." Susan steeled herself for the consequences. "Is that a problem?"

"Well yes and no. She wouldn't be the first human to find out about us. She'll have to be debriefed and all that stuff, but don't worry, it's not as bad as it sounds!" Les paused, a silence falling between them, "But right now we've got something a bit more pressing than politics. Remember the criminal we're after?"

Susan's blood ran cold.

"We didn't get to talk much about him, but because of your awakening, we think there's a chance his victim will be someone close to you. I don't want you to panic, but better safe than sorry. You said Anna ran off, do you know where she went?"

Susan looked down the street. There was no sign of her. "I... I don't know, she ran off, but she doesn't want to talk to me right now. Even if I found her, she might run away again... not that I couldn't catch her but..."

"Calm down Sue. I want you to look around and see if you can find her, but don't go too far. Tell me where you are and Evee and I will meet you there in a heartbeat!"

Susan could hear a car revving up in the background as she gave Les directions. There was no time to waste. The hunt was on.

CHAPTER 9
GAME OVER

Anna hadn't run far before she slowed to a walk, choking down gulps of air between sobs. Her throat burned in the frigid air. She couldn't imagine why anyone would ever run for fun. Her legs quivered beneath her, threatening to give out their support, but Anna forced one foot in front of the other, until her ragged breathing evened out. She stumbled, but caught herself, holding her body upright, even though she wanted to collapse on the ground. A chill spread over her skin and she stopped, looking over her shoulder the way she had come. The street was empty.

"Of course... why would she follow me after that?" The silence surrounding her swallowed her voice. Anna wrapped her arms across her chest and continued to walk away from home. The thought of going back and facing Susan was too much. This wasn't anything like how she'd imagined coming out to her best friend. Not at all. Her chest tightened as she fought back tears. She'd made a huge mess of things.

Anna found herself wandering down a trail that led to a nearby park. It was a small lot of sand hosting aging equipment. Slowly, everything was being replaced with plastic, but the old metal swing set still sat in place. Multiple layers of vibrant paint, peeled from the supports, exposing rust underneath. Anna took the long chains in hand and lowered herself onto a swing. The hinges at the top groaned in protest, but eased into a light creak as she swayed back and forth. Anna leaned a cheek against the cool chain, kicking off against the sand, listening to the sighing metal echo through the playground. She took her feet from the ground, letting the swing support her.

The crunch of footsteps across the sand startled her. Anna craned her neck to see who was coming. Her heart sank when she saw Will approaching her. He was the last person in the world she wanted to see right now. The hairs on the back of her neck prickled and the chill she had warded off earlier returned. The chains from the swing bit into her hands and she had to remember to relax her grip.

Will lifted his hand in greeting, but his step faltered and he hesitated. He smiled at Anna, but cast his eyes to the sand as he drew closer. He approached the swing next to her. "Mind if I join you?"

"It's a public park..." Anna replied, as frigid as the air.

Will lowered himself onto the swing facing the opposite direction and pushed himself back a little so he could see Anna's face. "Are you OK?"

Anna opened her mouth but no retort came out. Instead she shook her head. "I want to be left alone right now." She bit her lip to prevent herself from crying in front of Will.

"I'm sorry."

"What?" Anna struggled to reconcile those words coming from Will. Maybe she misheard him.

"I'm sorry," Will repeated, this time louder and clearer. He turned his gaze to his lap. "I'm bugging you again aren't I? You looked sad, so I thought you might want some company. If you want I can go."

"Don't be silly. It's alright," Anna's manners kicked in.

Will was far from his usual obnoxious self. Maybe this would be a good opportunity to set things straight. "I'm kind of dealing with a lot of stress right now."

"I know, I think we all are. I still can't believe Jim's gone. It puts things into perspective, doesn't it?" Will tried to say something but faltered. Instead he kicked at the sand. "Anna, I'm sorry if I've been a jerk to you. I just wanted to say that. I won't bother you anymore." He pushed himself off of the swing and began walking away.

"Wait!" Anna struggled to process everything that was happening, wishing the world would stand still for a moment so she could sort things out. Reconciliation with Will floated within her grasp. She couldn't let it go that easily. Anna tore herself from the swing, racing around to catch up to Will. He continued walking, but slowed down so Anna could catch up. "Wait... you're really sorry? Just like that?"

"That's what I said wasn't it?" Will's cheeks flushed.

"Oh... thank you. That means a lot to me." Anna crossed her arms over her chest once more, trying to fend off the cold by holding herself tight. "I'm sorry too, for being rude and the fighting... I didn't mean to... it's... everything is so messed up right now! I don't know what to say."

"Well it's good to know you don't hate me."

"Hate you?" Anna couldn't believe her ears. "I don't hate anyone! Why would you think that?"

"Because every time I try to talk to you, you get your back up about something."

"I wouldn't have to get defensive if you'd talk to me like a human being, like you're doing right now. Is that so hard?"

Will shrugged. "I guess it's hard to be human sometimes. All I wanted was to get your attention."

"Well, you got it, though I can't say it was a pleasant experience."

"I get that now, and I'm sorry. I guess I don't know what to say either. I've never had a problem saying the right thing to a girl before, but you're different Anna."

"Yeah... about that..." Anna searched for the right words to let Will down easy. She didn't want to ruin the understanding they were developing, but at the same time she didn't want Will to think she was interested. "Look..."

"I like you Anna." Will beat her to it.

Their footsteps echoed in the silence that followed.

Will stopped walking, staring intently at Anna. "It's OK. You don't have to say anything. I get it."

The hairs on the back of Anna's neck prickled but she brushed the feeling aside. Will took a step closer. He had a strange look in his eyes that wasn't there a moment ago. A look that caused the chill in Anna's spine to intensify into a shiver. Something was wrong.

"It doesn't really matter anymore," Will said, his voice cold, almost bored. Suddenly his face distorted into a wicked grin. "I'm afraid we've run out of time."

$$\Psi$$

Anna found herself on a cold, dusty floor. The room smelled of treated wood and chalky drywall. The last rays of sun scraped through the single window, casting long shadows through the room. It was getting dark. Anna tried to move but her muscles felt like they had been turned to stone. Feeling came to her limbs slowly as she stretched out.

She had no idea where she was. Everything had happened so fast. Will had moved so fast. Unnaturally fast. He moved with a strength and speed Anna knew wasn't possible, at least not for a human. Her mind snapped back to her conversation with Sue. She had said there were "others." If her best friend was a werewolf, then anything was possible.

Anna gripped her throbbing head, forcing herself to focus. It didn't matter, only survival mattered. She had to get away from Will. As she pushed herself up from the floor a cold voice called from the shadows.

"Don't try to run. There's no point."

Anna's blood went cold. Despite the warning, she sprinted toward the only door in the room. A shadow tore itself from the wall, moving faster than her eye could catch, and then Will was standing in front of her, blocking the exit.

"I told you. There's no point in trying to run." Will crossed his arms, leaning against the door frame. Despite his relaxed posture, there was a hungry glint in his eye.

Anna took a step back, weighing her options. Whatever Will was, he could move faster than her without breaking a sweat. Running really wasn't an option. Frantically, she looked around the room, for anything that might help her, but aside from some discarded *Tim's* cups, the room was empty. There was only the door and the single window for escape and judging by the view, they were on the second floor. Anna began to shake. There was no way out.

"What do you want?"

Will straightened up. A devilish twitch played across his lips that could have been a smile if it didn't look so threatening. "Good, you're coming around. Clearly, you can't escape, so it's better to accept things as they are."

"Why are you doing this?" Anna fought the panic tightening her throat.

Will took a step towards her, then another. Anna froze as he approached.

"You've been so much fun these past few months," he said. "It's a shame we can't go on. Alas, the game is drawing to a close and I'm rushed to end it."

Will came right up to her, breathing in heavily before circling Anna. He lifted a hand to caress Anna's shoulder. She flinched.

"What are you doing!?" She could no longer hide the fear in her voice.

"Having my fun! Just because I had to speed up the hunt doesn't mean I have to rush the finale."

"You're sick!"

Will laughed, "You have no idea, but then you're about to find out, aren't you?"

"No!" Anna tried to back away but Will caught her arm and slammed her into the floor.

Will stood over her, calmly waiting for her next reaction. Anna froze, but her body betrayed her as it started to tremble.

"See, I knew you were a smart one, but then I only chase smart ones. Those vapid high school girls can be so boring, but then once in a while there's one worth hunting!"

"Some hunter," Anna spat back, "You could at least give me a sporting chance!"

"You are absolutely delightful Anna! Do you know that?" Will bent down, reaching out a hand to cup Anna's cheek. "It's almost a waste to destroy you."

"Then why do it?" Anna jumped at the shred of hope. "Why not let me go?"

"Ah dear girl, if only I could, but it's all part of the game. A game I always win. Unfortunately, circumstances beyond my control have forced me a little ahead of schedule."

"Sounds like you're cheating to me."

"Ha! You are exceptional! I haven't had this much fun in nearly a hundred years."

"A hundred... what?"

"Oh no, no, no... I don't mean to stretch your fragile human mind, but I'm sure some part of you understands I'm not really human. Especially seeing as how you like to play with dogs."

"What are you?" Anna barely let her breath escape.

"So curious... maybe I'll keep you guessing to the end."

"What are you... going to do?"

"Well, make no mistake darling, this is the end, but I have this dreadful habit of playing with my food." Will licked his lips, running his eyes over Anna's body.

Anna shivered in revulsion, "You're disgusting."

Will leapt on top of her, straddling her hips and pinning her wrists to the floor. "You're a difficult woman, you know that?"

"Shut up! Get off me!"

Will smothered her screams with his lips. Anna went rigid. This couldn't be happening.

Will pulled back from his crushing kiss, then lowered his face again, gently pulling on Anna's lower lip. A needle of pain bit into it and the coppery taste of blood filled her mouth. Will's movements became wilder and more feral as he lapped at the blood pooling from the wounded lip. He kissed Anna deeply, forcing his tongue into her mouth.

Anna shuddered but she couldn't move. Her body didn't want to respond. In a fit of panic she took Will's tongue and bit down as hard and fast as she could. It was rewarding to feel Will flinch in pain. He drew back raising a hand to his now bloody mouth, and began to laugh.

"Oh, this... this is funny! It's too bad I don't have time to explain why, because this is hilarious."

Anna spat as more blood pooled in her mouth, but now there was something else. Will's blood had a bitter taste to it. Her stomach lurched as she struggled to get the sickening taste of him out of her mouth. Then her lip began to burn. That little pinprick which had almost become numb to pain suddenly felt like it was on fire. "I don't find this funny at all."

"No, and here I had so much planned for us, but now you've gone and ruined it! Silly girl. We can't take our time any longer. I'm afraid I'll have to finish this immediately." Will leaned forward again, but this time he placed his lips over Anna's neck.

CHAPTER 10
FIGHT FOR YOUR RIGHT

Susan paced back and forth on the empty street in front of her car. It was the last place she'd seen Anna and she didn't want to move from that spot. Les told her to stay put, but she couldn't sit still, instead she walked around her car as she waited for the cavalry. She heard the Hornet long before it pulled down the street. The screech of tires sounded out of place in the quiet subdivision.

As the Hornet pulled up to her, Susan ran toward it. Les barely stepped out the car before Susan flung herself at him, burying her tear stained face into his shoulder. "This is all my fault! If anything happens to Anna I'll never forgive myself!"

Les stroked her hair. "We're here now. Everything will be alright, I promise."

"Not to alarm anyone, but time is of the essence," Evee called from the driver's seat. "Sue, is there somewhere we can leave the car so we can... *change*?"

Susan pulled herself away from Les, dragging her sleeve across her face. "There's a park around the corner. I doubt anyone will be there now."

"Good, hop in!"

"Are you sure it's OK to leave..."

"We need a little privacy." Evee sniffed the air. "Plus we can run faster as wolves, and there's nothing stopping us from coming back here. We need to get you grounded if you're going to be any use to us."

"Me?" Susan scrambled into the car. "What can I do?"

"You know what Anna smells like," Les drew his seatbelt across his chest as Evee turned the car around. "You're our best hope for tracking her."

"But, I've never done that before!" Susan panicked. "I don't know how!"

"You do!" Les' faith didn't waver. "You just have to find her scent and we can help you. She's your best friend right? You'll know her scent when you find it."

Guilt lurched in Susan's stomach. "Some best friend I am."

"This isn't your fault Sue."

"I beg to differ."

"So you guys had a fight. It happens, but what Hunter does, if he does anything, is way beyond your control. Trust the good person that you are, and things will sort themselves out." Les' conviction was enough to make Susan want to believe what he said, no matter how ridiculous it sounded.

Evee parked the car in a little lot next to the playground. The sun was getting lower in the sky and the streetlights were turning on, casting their yellow light across the pavement.

Susan startled when both Les and Evee began removing their clothes with out a word. "Uh..."

"This is no time to be shy Sue." Evee took on an air of command. "Change and shift."

Les was out the door in a flash, with Evee right on his tail, before Susan even got her coat off. She tore off the rest of her clothes and willed herself to change. It happened easily, but she found herself staring at the car door handle, her breath misting the window. *Maybe I should have opened the door first?*

As if reading her mind, the door opened. Susan jumped out.

"I thought you might need a hand!" Les waved to her in his hybrid form before leaping into the bushes at the roadside, smoothly shifting into a full coyote in mid air.

Show off. Susan could barely walk in her wolf form, she had no idea how she was going to track someone. She loped off into the bushes after Les, and found Evee sitting and waiting for them, her fur a dull grey in the fading light.

"OK Sue, we're going to walk slowly back toward the spot you last saw Anna. Keep your nose to the ground for her scent. If you find it let out a howl and let us know. Can you do that?"

Susan wasn't sure but nodded anyway. They needed to hurry up and find Anna's trail before it was too late. Susan made her way back up the street, Les and Evee trailing behind. Putting her nose to the asphalt, she inhaled deeply. An assault of smells clogged her nostrils, causing Susan to cough. She took a step back. She had no idea what she was doing. She would never find Anna among all these odors.

Les came up beside her, sitting back on his haunches. He nodded, silently reminding Susan that she could do this. Taking a deep breath to clear her head, Susan closed her eyes, willing herself to calm down. Running around panicking wasn't going to help the situation.

She stood there a moment, at the edge of the park, getting her bearings when it came to her. One sweet smell rose above the rest. It was familiar. Susan put her nose to the ground. No, it wasn't in front of her. She swung around, her head weaving side to side, catching hints of the scent then losing it. It faded in and out of her nose with each sniff until she came to a spot where she was certain she had found it. Lifting her head to the sky Susan cried out. Les and Evee were already at her side. She had done it. She had found Anna's trail. All she needed to do was relax and trust her instincts.

Evee took up the trail, circling closer and closer toward the park. Suddenly her ears flattened against her skull and her lips drew back revealing teeth. She darted around the swing set, snarling and huffing at the sand underfoot. When she looked up, her eyes were the coldest Susan had ever seen them. Evee bolted back toward the car. Something was wrong. Susan stumbled, trying to keep up, but she heard Evee loud and clear when she reached the car. "I'm calling FENRIS. It's him!"

Ψ

Hunter's trail led to a part of the subdivision where new houses were being built. Thankfully that meant there were no humans around to contend with. More agents had been called in to back up the Burns siblings. Everyone was dressed in black swat gear, some as humans and some as the odd shaped hybrids Susan was getting used to. The only one not wearing the strange gear was Evee who paced along the bushes at the edge of the suburb where they were setting up for the strike. She looked like a strange apparition, a white wolf walking on two legs. Les crouched behind a bush, his hybrid nose digging through an old leather case that looked like an old fashioned doctor's bag. He wore the vest and dark clothes but refused any weapons or gear other than the bag.

Orders were issued and the operatives dispersed into the night except Les and Evee who were to take point from the bushes, and a human Susan who was told to stay put. It had only been a minute since the others had gone out but Evee shook with impatience, waiting for the operatives to get in position.

Susan's heart ached. She wanted to go with them, no matter what danger lay in the house, but everyone kept telling her to stay behind. "Couldn't I just follow one of you?"

"It's too dangerous!" Evee snapped at her. "Not just for you but for everyone. You can barely control your transformations!"

"I was in control enough to track! I won't get in your way, I promise. I'm not leaving Anna! Not now. Not after everything that's happened." To make a point, Susan shifted flawlessly into her wolf form and back again, managing to not get tangled her clothes. Stress somehow made the transformations easier.

Evee wheeled on her brother a hard edge taking over her voice, "Restrain her if you have to. I can't wait a second longer. I'm going in. I have to stop him." Evee shifted down onto four legs and snuck off toward the house.

"At least wait for the damn signal!" Les ran his fingers over his skull, pushing at his fur. "What am I going to do with you two! You both want to jump into this without thinking things through! We can't rush this. If we do, he could get away!"

Susan couldn't believe her ears. Everything she heard was about catching this Hunter. Nobody said anything about Anna. Maybe it was too late... No. If no one else was going to think about Anna, then it was up to her. She had to be the one. She had to be there for Anna no matter what. Susan focused on her body. It had become easier to shift back and forth, but she needed something more. She needed to be able to talk and fight. She needed the strongest parts of her wolf and human self, for Anna's sake. She needed to be a werewolf.

Muscles taught, Susan clenched her jaw forcing the change, but nothing happened. *Come, on. I need this! It has to work!* She realized she was holding her breath and Susan let out a gasp of air. She looked up at the darkening sky. The world around her had gone still. The calm before the storm. Closing her eyes, Susan searched her body for the beast she knew was there. *Come on, I need you. Please!*

Susan felt a dull ache in her heart. That ache began to rumble and suddenly she felt a familiar twitch to her body. It was like a normal shift, but different. Her blood seared through her veins and when she opened her eyes again she saw Les staring at her, his mouth hanging open.

"You did it! You hybridized!"

"Let's go." Susan surprised herself with the intensity of her own voice.

"This is such a bad idea..." Les snapped his bag shut. "Let's do it. Stay behind me at all times, and do what I tell you!"

Hope welled in Susan's chest. "Let's go save Anna!"

As they approached the house, Susan became aware of the other agents. There were teams at all the exits around the house, waiting to move in, waiting for the signal, whatever that might be.

A blaze of white flew through the air, launching itself from the ground up and through a second story window. Everything happened all at once. Screams filled the air among the shattering of glass. The night was alive with shadows moving in every direction toward the house.

Something dark fell from the window, or maybe it had jumped. It moved too fast for Susan to tell. It was followed immediately by a werewolf, shimmering white in the moonlight; a howling angel of death. The shadowy figure stood and Susan saw William Murry staring back at her, fear etched on his face. Evee lunged at him, grabbing for his neck, but she missed and buried her teeth in his shoulder. Will fought back clawing at the wolf's eyes, eventually slamming her against the wall of the house with so much force the wall caved in and she tumbled inside.

"What the Hell is going on?" Susan asked Les, but he was already moving. As promised, Susan followed like his shadow, into the house, up stairs, down a hall and into a scene from her worst nightmare. Anna lay on the floor, her neck torn to shreds.

Susan stumbled and the room tilted unnaturally. "No... No! Not again!" Visions of Jim lying before her with his throat torn out swam before her eyes, overlaying and melting into the scene before her. There was blood everywhere, the overwhelming stench of it burning Susan's nose. A ringing in her ears drowned out the noise and everything went fuzzy. Susan's face connected with the dusty hardwood floor. Her body went limp, refusing to respond to her urge to scream.

"She's turning!" A voice cut through the chaos.

"What?" Susan's mouth was dry, but control seeped back into her limbs.

"... heavy blood loss. I need back up and a blood source now!" Les yelled to another agent.

The room sharpened and Susan saw it clearly for the first time. Agents in black swat gear swarmed through the room and Les had his hands on Anna's neck staunching the bleeding. Susan got to her knees and crawled over to Les. "She's... alive?"

"Barely," Les' face was gaunt as he worked to close up the neck wound. "Even if I can fix this mess, and get a transfusion going, she's still..." he looked away from Susan. "She's got a long way to go."

"Why? How?" Susan grasped for something, anything that would tell her Anna would be alright.

"Grab me those scissors," Les nodded at his bag before becoming engrossed in the work of fixing Anna's neck. His fingers flew across the wound, fast and sure, weaving together something almost human again.

Les' calm determination infected Susan as she grabbed the scissors for him. "Can I help?"

"One sec." The boy didn't take his eyes from his patient. "Like I said, I can fix the wounds and give her blood, but she's turning."

"What the hell does that mean?"

"Hunter is a vampire. Unlike us, he can pass on his curse

to others. Here, hold this." Les placed Susan's hands over the gauze now covering Anna's wounded neck. "Apply pressure firmly, but not too hard. See the colour of her skin? Her eyes?"

Anna was terribly pale, but Susan assumed that was from blood loss. Then she saw Anna's eyes. Once soft and doe-like, they were now utterly black, rimmed with red.

"I don't know how or why, but he started the turning process while he was feeding on her. Turning is dangerous at the best of times... most don't survive."

"Don't say that!" Tears threatened, blurring Susan's vision. "What can we do?"

"I'm reluctant to do it, but I don't think we have a choice. Sue," Les held her arm in a firm grip, "I have to go find her, and bring her back to us. When Evee gets back, have her hook herself up for a transfusion. Don't worry, she knows how. And if I don't come back, tell her I love her."

"What... Where are you going?" Susan pleaded for an explanation. Nothing Les said made any sense.

"Don't worry, my body will be right here..."

"That doesn't tell me anything!"

"I know, I'm sorry. I... I'll tell you all about it when I get back."

"You better!" Susan threatened, not because she needed an explanation, but because she truly wanted Les to be alright.

"Oh, one more thing, once I'm under, talk to us. It might help us find our way back."

"I don't understand."

Les smiled, but it didn't reach his eyes. He pulled a needle and solution out of the medical bag, prepared a shot and injected himself in the arm. Carefully, he put the needle aside and sat cross legged on the floor above Anna's head. Placing one hand on either of Anna's temples, he lowered his head, his eyes lidded, half closed. As Susan watched, the focus of his eyes disappeared and they glazed over.

"Les? Are you OK?"

No response.

"Um, OK, so I guess I'll just sit here and talk then..."

The door to the room slammed into the wall as it was ripped off its hinges. Evee stormed into the room, her white fur marred with patches of red. However, when she saw Les bent over Anna, her ferocity melted. "No! No no no no no..." She crawled over to her brother, then spotted the needle and solution laying neatly beside him. "No!" she screamed. "Dammit Les, I won't let him take you too!"

"E... Evee?" Susan's voice was weak.

"What?" The fearsome white wolf reared its head, snapping its teeth at Susan.

As terrifying as Evee was in that moment, Susan saw past the snarling fangs. She was scared too. "Les told me to tell you something about starting a transfusion when you got here. He said you'd know how..."

For the first time, Evee looked at the girl lying on the floor. Her eyes widened and she brought her hand to her muzzle, catching a gasp. Evee's anger retreated, replaced with something Susan could only guess was sorrow. Evee traced a claw gingerly over Anna's cheek. "Yes. Of course." She turned and spoke to her brother, "You're right. I'm sorry. I panicked. He got away again! I'm so mad at myself, but you're right, this is more important right now."

Susan watched Evee rummage through Les's bag taking out needles and tubes. Soon, a line of crimson ran between the werewolf and Anna.

"You're so lucky to have a sister who's a universal donor you know that?"

"Um, are you talking to me?" Susan asked. The other agents had vacated the room on Evee's arrival.

"Did Les not tell you? We need to talk to them. It'll help them find their way back."

"He did say that, but I don't understand. Where are they?"

"I don't know to be honest. You'll have to get Les to explain it to you."

"Like a mind meld or something?"

"Ha! Not exactly. I can talk to Les, but I don't know your friend, so maybe you should talk to her."

"About what? We left off... badly."

"Then start there. Tell her how you feel."

Anna's face was getting paler and her eyes darker. Once in a while she would twitch or shake.

"Anna... I'm so sorry. Please forgive me. I know things have been crazy and I... I messed up. I should have been paying attention. I was so wrapped up in myself that I forgot you were struggling too. I'm sorry. Please come back. I don't think I could live without you. Please..."

Anna's body went rigid, then spasmed.

"What's going on? Evee?!" Susan searched the older woman for a comforting explanation.

Les let out a gasp and crumpled forward, panting as if from heavy exertion.

"Welcome back brother." A wry smile played across Evee's face, and she went to remove the tube connecting her to Anna. "Did you find her?"

Les shuddered, but he leaned back and nodded, "We're through the woods."

Anna began squirming at their feet.

"I'd get back if I were you." Les pushed Susan out of the way.

"Why..."

Anna rolled onto her side and vomited.

"That's why."

Anna's eyes fluttered open, and Susan saw the same soft brown irises she'd known for years.

"Oh my God! You're OK!" Susan scooped the smaller girl up in her arms.

"What happened?" Anna croaked. She tried to sit up on her own, but fell back against Susan.

"It's alright. You're safe now." Les leaned over, checking the gauze of her neck wound. "You're alive, but weak. Don't try to move. We'll take care of you. "

Anna stared at him, mouth half open, "I know you."

Les winked at her. "Smart girl."

Anna turned to Susan, "And you're here too! You're really here! I thought it was you, but I wasn't sure."

"You mean you heard me?"

"I heard your voice, but I don't remember what it said."

"I was telling you what a dumbass I've been and that I'm sorry... so, so, sorry."

"That's funny, I was thinking the same thing while I was dying." Colour surged into Anna's pale cheeks.

"We can move her now," Les said.

Evee got to her feet. "Let's get out of here."

"Right, let's get you two home!" Les said.

Susan cringed. "My mom..."

"Don't worry," Les picked up his bag, "This time we'll help you explain everything."

The tension in Susan's shoulders released. At least she wouldn't have to face her mother alone. She had a lot of explaining to do and she feared screwing things up even further. Wrapping one arm under Anna's knees and the other around her shoulders, Susan lifted the smaller girl. She was surprised how light Anna was. "I'm not crushing you with my super-strength or anything am I?"

"I think I'd let you know." Anna cuddled into Susan's fur, struggling to keep her eyes open.

Susan carried Anna out of the room and down the stairs, leaving the horrible house behind. "Listen Anna, I know you're tired but, I wanted to say, I understand why you were so mad. I let my problems take over and..."

"I know. I get it. So much has happened. Can we forget we ever had that stupid fight?"

"Done!" Susan was more than willing to put this mess

behind them, but she wanted to be clear, "Um... when you're feeling better though, I hope you'll want to talk to me about what you've been going through. It sounds like you've been struggling a lot and I think it's my turn to listen."

"Oh, *that*..." Anna squirmed, trying to curl herself into a ball to make herself invisible. She searched Susan's face, "Does that mean you're OK with me being... different?"

"Of course!" Susan said. "I love you Anna, no matter what you are... platonicly!"

"That's good." Anna relaxed, sinking into Susan's arms. "You're not my type anyway."

"Hey! What's that supposed to mean?!" Susan wasn't ready to give up their banter, not when everything was returning to normal, but Anna's eyes closed and her breathing deepened. She had succumbed to exhaustion.

CHAPTER 11
FAMILY AFFAIR

Mr. Russel nearly fainted when he opened the door to see Susan Wolfe carrying something resembling the corpse of his daughter.

"She's alright!" Susan said before he could question anything. "She's asleep and I don't want to wake her."

Mr. Russel stared. Anna was frighteningly pale with deep circles under her eyes and a gauze bandage wrapped around her neck. "What... what's going on?!"

"I'm sorry," Susan shifted Anna's weight in her arms, "But can we come in?"

Mr. Russel noticed others standing behind Susan. There was a boy around his daughter's age who seemed friendly enough, but the woman standing beside him wore a severe scowl on her face. Her pale eyes caught the light from the doorway, reflecting the way an animal's would in the dark. Mr. Russel rubbed his eyes. Worry and fatigue were making him see things.

A tall, well dressed man pushed forward extending his hand. "Mr. Russel? My name is Vincent Ravini, contact agent of FENRIS." He flashed an official badge by Mr.

Russel and continued. "I'm sorry we have to meet under these circumstances, but I'll explain everything to you fully."

"What happened?" Mr. Russel took a step back allowing Susan and her entourage through the door.

A squeal rang through the hallway as his wife approached, making a bee-line for Anna. "What's going on?! What happened to Anna? Is she alright?"

"She's fine Mrs. Russel," Susan let her inspect her daughter. "She passed out from exhaustion."

"Are you sure? Maybe we should take her to the hospital?"

Vincent was quick to interrupt, "She's been examined by one of our finest medical staff Mrs. Russel. I assure you, Anna will be fine, she just needs rest."

"I was going to put her to bed," Susan adjusted her grip and headed toward the stairs.

Mr. Russel realized how silly he was being with everyone standing in his doorway, especially Susan who's muscles must be giving out from carrying his daughter like that. "Take her upstairs would you please Susan? No need to stand around." He motioned the strangers toward the living room. "I'm sorry, I've forgotten my manners! What did you say you're name was Mr... ?"

"Ravini. But please, call me Vince."

"Right, Vince." Try as he might, Mr. Russel couldn't keep the edge off his voice, "And would you care to explain to me, Vince, how you showed up at my door in the middle of the night with my daughter in such a state?"

"I intend to explain everything Mr. Russel," Vince said. "However, it might take a while, and I appreciate your patience."

"Right, and you're with the police or CSIS or something?"

"FENRIS sir. You've likely never heard of us, we're sort of, off the books one might say."

"What does this have to do with Anna?" Mr. Russel sank into his favorite easy chair. The others took places around the living room as his wife and Susan returned from upstairs.

"Oh goodness!" Mrs. Russel wrung her hands together. "I wasn't expecting anyone! Would anyone like a cup of tea?"

"Tea!?" Mr. Russel felt his right eye pulse. "It's the middle of the night! Who wants tea?"

"Actually I'd love a cup right about now," the boy jumped up from his place on the couch. "Would you like a hand Mrs. Russel?"

"Leslie!" Vince was quick to scold him. "It's alright Mrs. Russel. Please don't trouble yourself. Do whatever you need to make yourself comfortable."

"I'll put the kettle on." Mrs. Russel made her way to the kitchen, Les in tow.

Mr. Russel rubbed the tension from his face, "Now you've got her going."

It took forever for the clanging of cutlery and china to subside, for the tea to brew and be poured and for everyone to finally be sitting quietly in the living room. Mr. Russel gripped the armrests of his chair, barely containing his growing anxiety. "So, is someone going to tell me now, what's going on?"

"Yes." Vince took a deep breath. "I'd like to start by saying your daughter will be alright. She's been through a lot tonight and needs her rest, but she will be fine."

"So you've said, but what happened?"

"I'd like to put your mind at ease Mr. Russel, but I'm afraid there is no simple version of the story I'm going to tell you. Please bear with me. As I mentioned, I'm here on behalf of an organization called FENRIS. Our job is to monitor certain individuals with a known medical condition. For the most part, these individuals are law abiding citizens, but once in a while, someone goes out on a limb and disobeys the law. Our job then is to track them down and bring them to justice as necessary."

"Are you trying to tell me, Vince, that my daughter had a run in with some sort of whack-job?"

"Mr. Russel, I know this is hard to hear, but please try not to jump to conclusions. It's not always this straightforward, but yes, in this case we are dealing with a criminal FENRIS has been hunting for many years."

"What did that creep do to my daughter?!" Mr. Russel was done being polite.

"Please, Mr. Russel, calm down. Anna is going to be fine. She did have contact with a criminal we call Hunter. He was going to harm Anna, but we interceded before anything serious happened."

"Then why is she passed out like that? You can't tell me nothing happened. What did he do to her?"

"Mr. Russel, I understand you are very upset but please..."

"I want answers and I want them now!" Mr. Russel slammed his fist into the arm of his chair.

Vince folded his hands in front of him, choosing his words carefully. "Anna was targeted by Hunter. She was going to be his next murder victim. He abducted Anna this afternoon, but we managed to find them before he could reach his goal. Anna was injured, but our medical team has attended to her. It could have been worse, Mr. Russel, far worse."

Mr. Russel's mouth was dry but he forced the words out, "*How* was she injured?"

Vince shifted, visibly uncomfortable. "The nature of Anna's injury is complicated. I'm not sure you're ready to hear it."

"What the Hell does that mean? Stop beating around the bush and spit it out!"

"Anna was bitten by Hunter. She was lucky to survive."

"What kind of nut-case bites people?!"

"A vampire." Vince remained serious, his voice deadpan. Silence reigned in the room.

Mr. Russel tittered in an uneasy laugh. "Wait, are you trying to tell me, this sicko thinks he's some kind of vampire?"

"No, I'm telling you he *is* a vampire. He kills his victims by draining their blood. That's what he tried to do to Anna, however, a complication arose..."

"No no no." Mr. Russel rose from his seat, pacing the living room floor. "You're not going to sit there and try to tell me my daughter was attacked by a vampire. This is beyond ridiculous! I don't care who you are, or who you work for, get out of my house!"

"I can see you're upset. This is probably not the best time to talk about this." Vince rose from his seat, straightening his jacket. "I will be in touch with you."

"Oh no you won't! I've had enough of your shenanigans!" Mr. Russel pointed an accusing finger at Vince, his voice rising to a scream, "Get out!"

Suddenly the room whirled before him as a hand clamped around Mr. Russel's neck tearing him from the ground so that his feet dangled beneath him. He choked and spluttered, fighting to regain balance until the horrifying visage of a white wolf snarled into his face.

"You should be grateful, your daughter is alive, not cursing the people who saved her!"

The hand around his neck released and Mr. Russel crumpled to the floor. He reached a protective hand up to his neck while frantically casting about the living room, but there was no sign of the strange creature. "What... what was that?"

"That was Evelyn Burns." Vince rubbed long, elegant fingers into his temples. "Please excuse my associate's behavior. It's been a hard night for everyone."

Vince held out his hand to help Mr. Russel to his feet, but the older man waved him away. "Just go, please! I... I don't want any trouble."

"I'm sorry Mr. and Mrs. Russel. This is not how I intended to explain things. I think we should go." Vince nodded at the boy and Susan, who rose and made their way to the door.

The silence the guests left in their wake was disconcerting. Mr. Russel sat beside his wife on the sofa. She leaned into him letting out a sob. He held her tight, letting out the tears he had been holding back all evening.

Ψ

Anna ran her fingers through silky white fur. Her bed was snug and she felt warm cuddled up to the white wolf lying next to her. It smelled wonderful and familiar, even though Anna couldn't remember where it came from. Perhaps it had always been there, watching over her as she slept. But something itched in the back of her mind. She had seen the wolf somewhere else, somewhere unpleasant. Anna's neck throbbed and her limbs twitched. A fire was spreading from her mouth through the rest of her body. She clawed at her skin, but the burning ran deeper, through her veins. She tried to cry out, but couldn't move. No longer in her bed, she lay on a cold, dusty floor. The window above her was shattering in slow motion, flecks of glass flying in every direction. The white wolf flew through a spray of shards, her lips drawn back in a terrible snarl.

Anna bolted upright, her heart hammering in her chest. Familiar walls surrounded her and she realized she was in her room. She placed a hand over the thumping in her chest, feeling her heart slam against her ribs. At least it was beating. She must be alive after all. Slowly she brought her hand from her chest up to her neck. Her fingers grazed a bandage and she drew them back in shock. Memories trickled back to her as she carefully inspected the spot where Will had bitten her. It was sore, but not painful, a dull ache instead of the fire she had been dreaming of.

Anna tugged at the tape holding the gauze to her neck. This wasn't a dream. It was real. She almost died last night. She could feel the veil of darkness closing in around her, but then someone saved her. Someone pulled her back from the abyss in the nick of time and lead her back to the world of the living. It was hard to remember, like trying to recall a dream once you wake up. Maybe it was all in her head, something her mind concocted while she was dying, but there was a lingering sense – even now in the waking world – that it had been all too real. Someone led her through the darkness, then she heard Susan calling her. The next thing Anna knew, she was lying on her side, face to face with a strange wolf creature with fur tinted the same colour as Susan's hair. Despite never having seen Susan like that before, there was no doubt in Anna's mind who she was looking at.

There were others too, so many strangers clad in black, but one stood out. A boy with kind eyes. He was smaller than the others, more like a coyote than a wolf, but Anna found herself drawn to him. The way he smelled and moved reminded her of the being who had pulled her from the darkness. It was as if that essence had taken shape and realized itself in front of her.

A soft knock on the door startled Anna. She smoothed the sheets around her, before calling at whoever it was to come in.

The door opened and a boy, no older than herself entered. Anna stared. It was him. Even as a human she could tell it was the coyote from the night before and the essence from the dark. Anna felt her face grow hot when she realized she was staring.

"Oh good, you're awake!" The boy moved with an easy grace over to her bedside. "I thought you might be, but I didn't want to wake you if you weren't."

Anna looked up, searching his eyes. "You're the one from last night aren't you?"

Shock spread across his face, but then he laughed. "I won't be able to hide anything from you. I'm Les."

"Anna."

"I know who you are believe it or not, and I've come

to check up on you." Les plopped himself on the foot of her bed, placing a leather medical bag between them. He rummaged through it, pulling out a stethoscope. "Don't worry, I'm a doctor."

Coming from anyone else, Anna would have taken it as a joke, but even with Les making light of his position, she knew it was true. She believed him without question, feeling there was more to this boy than met the eye. It felt odd to trust a stranger so wholeheartedly, but Anna did.

Les ran his fingers over Anna's wrist, taking her pulse. "You gave us quite a scare last night."

"Sorry about that." Anna cringed, trying to withdraw.

"Don't be, it wasn't your fault."

"So, it was you, when I was dying..." Anna studied the strange boy. "I was dying right?"

"Yes and no." Les occupied himself by checking over her neck instead of meeting her eyes. "You suffered heavy blood loss, but if you're talking about the place we met, that's something else."

"So it was real? I didn't dream it or make it up?"

"It's very real. You went through a lot last night." Les leaned over her, removing the gauze from her neck. "You might have a bit of a scar."

"Only a bit? That's a small price to pay."

"The price is greater than you think." Les sounded too grave to be giving her a clean bill of health.

"What do you mean?"

"Well," Les sat back, making himself comfortable, "I know you know about werewolves, but do you know what Will was and what he did to you?"

Revulsion shook Anna's body. "He was a creep! But I'm guessing he was something else too?" Anna brought her fingers to the wound on her neck. It felt closed, but there was no way it could have knitted so quickly. "I'm guessing vampire?"

"Bingo!"

"Do I win a prize?" Sarcasm felt like the only thing keeping her from going over the edge.

"Actually, sort of." Les placed a finger on the spot on Anna's lip where Will had bitten her. "What happened here?"

Memories Anna didn't want to remember flashed before her eyes. She tried to speak but her throat felt like it was closing.

"Oh!" Les drew back giving Anna space. "You don't have to say anything if you don't want to, but I'm here to listen if you do."

"That was where he started." Words tumbled out of Anna's mouth and she touched the spot on her lip, now a small bump. "He bit me there before he did this," she pointed at her neck. The memories flashed through her mind, fresh and raw and she had to hold her hands together on her lap to keep them from shaking. "He laughed at me at one point. He said it was funny but he didn't have time to explain. He... kissed me." Anna blanched. "I couldn't move. I couldn't think of anything to do, so I bit his tongue as hard as I could. That's when he laughed at me."

"Ah," Les said slowly, "It's starting to make sense now. You're a brave girl Anna, and I'm really sorry for everything that happened to you last night."

Anna could no longer hold back the tears and hunched forward into a sobbing ball. Les placed his hand on hers, lightly, ready to pull back, but Anna grabbed it, clutching it between her own. She leaned forward into the boy and he held her as she cried.

Eventually the tears stopped and her trembling subsided. "Sorry, I didn't mean to do that."

"It's fine. If you ever want to talk about it, I'll be there for you."

"Even though we just met?"

"Well, our first meeting was special. Once you've seen someone's essence, you know their heart. I liked what I saw in the dark place. I assume you liked me too."

"I did, but um... not in a way... uh..."

Les laughed. "Relax Anna, I didn't mean 'liking' in a romantic context. I've seen your true heart remember, I get it. I understand your not into guys that way."

"Really? How did you know?"

"Takes one to know one maybe?" Les winked at her. "Or maybe I can tell from experience. I think I'll keep you guessing."

"You're such a tease."

"See, you know my heart too!"

Anna narrowed her eyes at the boy, as if squinting would allow her to see that nagging thread she was grasping for, but the clue didn't come from anything visual, instead the answer bubbled up from her heart, "You're bi right?"

Les drew back, his brows lifting in shock, but his easy grin returned along with a bit of colour to his cheeks, "I'm not going to be able to hide anything from you am I?"

Anna laughed from sheer relief. Les was easy to talk to and he was right, she did know him rather intimately already. She trusted him. "So can I ask you something then? When Will said my biting him was funny, was that because he was a vampire?"

"That is kind of funny, but I don't think that's what he meant. When you drew his blood and exposed it to your own, you started a process we call turning. It's how vampires change a human into a vampire."

"So I started turning myself into a vampire?"

"Yup. Completely by accident. That's what sent you into the darkness. By helping you find your way back, we completed the process. If we hadn't, you would have died."

Anna shuddered, "Would I have stayed in that dark place?"

"I'm not sure to be honest. There's a lot we don't know about death or the darkness."

"So, did I die last night? Am I... undead?"

"No. I assure you, you're quite alive, but you're also a vampire."

"What does that mean?"

"You're about to find out." Les pulled a plastic bag out from his medical case that looked an awful lot like a blood bag. "Time for breakfast!"

CHAPTER 12
OPPORTUNITY KNOCKS

A plethora of voices came from Anna's living room. She wasn't sure what she had expected, but it wasn't this. Her parents and Susan's mother were present, but there were a couple of faces she didn't recognize, namely a tall man in a suit and a stern woman with cold blue eyes. Anna caught her breath. She knew those eyes. They were the same as the white wolf's from her nightmare. Or was it a memory?

Les gave her a nudge with his elbow. "Don't worry she doesn't bite... often!"

Anna blushed, embarrassed to be caught staring. Even though she wasn't paying them any attention, the voices from the living room kept finding their way to her ears and for some reason the smell of all those people became overwhelming.

"Anna, are you OK?"

She opened her eyes to see Les reaching out as if to steady her. Anna had been holding her ears with her hands. Sounds kept coming in waves, but they were starting to quiet. "I'm fine, I think. I don't know. Everything got really loud for a second."

"Don't worry, you'll get used to it."

"So this is normal?"

"Your senses are adjusting. You'll find yourself sensitive to noise, smells, light..." Les checked her again. "Let me know if you feel sick or anything."

Anna balled her hands into fists, waiting for her senses to overload again, but nothing happened. "I'm fine now. We can go in."

Anna followed Les into the living room, slowly taking everything in. A shaggy, golden werewolf bounded over to greet her, wrapping her arms around Anna.

"I'm glad you're alright!" Susan held her tight.

"So am I!" Anna hugged her back, happy to be in the company of her friends and family.

"If everyone wouldn't mind taking a seat," the tall man in the neat suit addressed the room, "Now that we're all present, we have some things to discuss." As everyone took a seat he made his way over to Anna, extending his hand, "I'm glad you could join us Anna. I'm Vince. It's a pleasure to meet you."

Anna shook his hand, wanting to melt into the background once again, but curiosity made her hang on a little longer. Les had told her there was another vampire who would be helping them sort things out. Anna wasn't sure what to expect after her first encounter with a vampire, but Vince seemed kind enough.

Vince let Anna escape to a seat on the couch between Susan and her mom. Anna shot a glance at the woman with the pale eyes who was sitting away from her, near the kitchen, but she made no move to introduce herself.

Vince cleared his throat, drawing everyone's attention. He stood at the end of the living room, ready to make a speech, "Thank you all for being here. I know the last few days have been trying for everyone. At the best of times, introducing families to our world is a stressful matter, so considering the circumstances, you're all adjusting quite well. I'm used to inducting families under far less trauma," Vince paused, flashing a glare at the blue eyed woman in the corner. "So I appreciate your patience. My job is to help make this transition as smooth as possible, so if there's anything I can do for you, please don't hesitate to ask."

"Maybe we should bring our newest arrival up to speed?" Les motioned to Anna.

Her head was swimming, "How long was I out for?"

"Nearly a full day," Les told her.

"We were so worried!" Her mother reached over and stroked Anna's hair.

She leaned into her mother, "I'll be alright. I feel fine actually."

"That's good, but things have changed sweetie. Things are going to be different from now on." Her mother's gaze grew distant.

Anna thought of the 'breakfast' she had eaten and the ringing in her ears as her senses adjusted. Things would be different, but they would find a way to manage.

"It pains me to say it," Vince said, "But this case is going to be drastically different."

"Why?" Something gnawed at the back of Anna's mind. There was a piece of the puzzle everyone else could see, but she was missing.

"Anna, it pains me to tell you that the man who attacked you escaped our agents last night. He's still at large."

The room began to swim and Anna felt light-headed, "But... I saw him fighting with a white wolf! He was thrown out a window!"

"That was me." All eyes went to the woman at the back of the room. "I was the werewolf you saw fighting with him. I had him, but he slipped out of my grasp." She clutched her fists tightly. "I'm sorry."

"Evee don't blame yourself for what happened..." Vince soothed her.

"I had him Vince! We had him! All this suffering should have ended last night, but it didn't."

"So he got away," Susan huffed, crossing her arms over her chest, "Good riddance!"

"I wish it were that simple," Vince tented his fingers, pursing his lips, pausing to choose his next words.

Fear gripped Anna. "It's not over is it? He'll come back."

The room went silent, collectively holding its breath until Vince spoke. "No. It's not over. Not as long as Anna's alive."

The room erupted into dismay. Everyone was shouting all at once. Anna clamped her hands over her ears and squeezed her eyes shut, but she couldn't drown it out. Worse was the growing fear spreading from her gut, making her blood run cold. Panic began to take over. There was no way out. Will would come for her.

A hand on her knee brought the room back into focus. "Anna, are you OK? Do you need to go some place quiet?" Les' presence was stabilizing.

"I'll be fine if everyone stops shouting!" Anna massaged her temples and the room quieted.

"There's no need to be alarmed," Vince said. "I know the situation sounds dire, but we actually have the upper hand."

"How?" Anna's father grumbled from his easy chair.

"I'm saying we're in a good position. Anna is safe, and under our care we have a chance to catch and dispose of Hunter – or Will as you knew him – once and for all."

Vince's confidence failed to reassure everyone.

"What are you suggesting exactly?" Anna's father narrowed his eyes, studying Vince.

"This is all an elaborate game to Hunter," Vince explained, "But his obsession will be his undoing! In his mind, he never loses, he'll merely see this game as unfinished. Meaning he'll return to finish what he started. But because we know his target is Anna, we can protect her, even go so far as to draw Hunter into a trap!"

"You really think he'll fall for something like that?" Anna's father scoffed.

"He will." Les spoke up. "He's never 'lost' to us before and last night was a big blow to his ego."

"But have you ever done this before? How do you know it will work?!"

"Nothing is certain Mr. Russel," Les suddenly looked older than his years, as if a lifetime had been added to his features. "But the best chance your daughter has to live is to put her in FENRIS' care."

"First you fail to protect her, then you let this nut-case get away, and now I'm supposed to hand over my only child to you for her 'protection?' Forget it!"

"Please hear me out," Vince took back the floor. "The safest place in the country for any werewolf or vampire child is at a private academy that I head. That's why I'm here and not some other delegate of FENRIS. Our grounds are one hundred percent FENRIS monitored and we can comfortably house the extra security and operations needed in this situation. It's the safest place for the girls right now."

"Wait," Mrs. Wolfe spoke up, "What do you mean 'girls?' Is Susan in trouble too?"

"In a manner of speaking," Vince said. "Susan has been summoned by FENRIS for an evaluation concerning her involvement in the death of James Schenn."

"It doesn't rain but it pours," Susan groaned.

"Yes and rather than separating our resources it makes sense to all meet in one place."

"I don't know," Mrs. Wolfe wrung her hands together. "This is all happening so fast! I feel like my head might explode!"

"You're not the only one," Anna's mother assured her. "It's too much to take in all at once! I don't know what to say, much less do!"

"Where are we going?" Susan asked. Her mother glared at her.

"It's outside of Ottawa. We have many acres of estate and excellent facilities. It's called the Red Oak Institute and it was designed as a private school where werewolves and vampires could go to learn and develop their gifts."

"So we're going to Hogwarts?" Susan's lips drew back in a wolfish grin.

"If I had a nickel..." Vince smoothed a stray hair that had fallen from his immaculate head. "You are more than welcome to join us, even under normal circumstances."

"I don't know about this," Mrs. Wolfe said. "Even under 'normal' circumstances I'd be reluctant to allow Susan to go."

Evee stepped forward, "Mrs. Wolfe, and Mr. and Mrs. Russel, I know you've been through a lot. It would be hard for anyone to put their trust in a bunch of strangers, but I want you all to know that I'm willing to commit myself to the lives of your children, by making them my own. I'm willing to adopt them into my pack."

Vince and Les went silent, their eyes wide.

"What does that mean?" Mrs. Wolfe asked.

Vince found his voice though he continued to stare at Evee, "To werewolves, their pack is a sacred bond. It's like a family, though the members don't have to be related by blood. It connects the members to each other. It's actually quite an honor that Evelyn is offering this to your daughters."

Evee knelt in front of Mrs. Wolfe, "It means what is mine is theirs and that I will have only their best interests at heart. It means I will protect them at any cost and love them as my own family."

"That's some pretty heavy stuff," Susan swallowed.

"It is," Evee said, "But we've already been through so much together. I ask your parent's for their permission, but the choice is yours."

Susan answered without hesitation, "You've been there for me when I needed you most. I can't imagine having anyone else at my back through this craziness. I accept! If it's OK with you Mom?"

Mrs. Wolfe flung her hands in the air, "I don't know Sue! You're old enough to decide who your friends are!"

"Thanks Mom!"

Evee turned to Anna, her pale eyes welling with concern, "I know we haven't spoken..."

"I remember you." The vision of the terrifying white wolf flying through the window was tempered with memories of a loving voice calling through the darkness. Evee had been there when Anna woke up. She had saved her life. Anna's body went warm. There was already a special connection, even though they hadn't spoken to each other in the waking world. "I'll accept too."

"Sweetie, are you sure?" Her mother gripped her hand.

"Out of the question!" Her father's face flared red.

"Mum, Dad, I've never been more sure of anything my whole life." Anna was taken aback by her own confidence, but she stood by what she said.

"If this is what you want..."

"This is insane!" Her father folded his arms across his chest, clearly unhappy, but one look at his daughter was enough to make him cave in. "Do what you want."

"There's just a small formality to make things final then." Evee bent her head to her forearm. Her teeth elongated and in one fluid motion she pierced her skin. She motioned for Susan to do the same.

Susan awkwardly bit into her arm. She flinched and a trickle of bright red blood flowed from her wrist. Evee took her arm, placing the wounds together, letting the blood mingle.

"Is that even sanitary!?" Anna's mother paled.

No one else made a sound.

"I Evelyn Burns take into my pack, you Susan Wolfe. Our blood is our bond, our strength is our family. I swear fealty to you. Do you make the same oath to me?"

"I do."

"Then it's done."

Susan leaned forward as if someone had punched her in the gut. She put a hand to her head. "What a rush!"

"It'll pass. Take it easy for now." Evee rose and knelt in front of Anna, putting her arm forward. "The same falls to you."

Anna brought her arm to her lips. She wasn't sure she'd be able to draw her own blood, but the sight and smell of it coming from Evee's arm made her feel strange and hungry. Her canines ached and when she brought them down to her skin, found they were longer and sharper than they should have been. They cut easily through her skin and Anna drew back, holding her bleeding arm out to Evee.

As their arms connected and their blood mixed, Anna felt a strange sensation. It was not unlike meeting Les in the darkness, except this time their essences were diluted by their physical bodies. Still, it was a raw and emotional connection. When she spoke her affirmation, Anna felt Evee's life force entwining with hers, but they weren't alone. Les and Susan were there too, and there were others she had never met. In one moment, she knew all of them intimately. Then they were gone. Anna gasped for air.

"Honey are you alright?" Her mother took ahold of her hand.

"Yeah," Anna managed to breathe out. "I'm fine."

"You will take care of her?" Anna's mother asked.

"Like my own family," Evee gave her a kind smile, sincere enough to melt the hardest heart.

"With that settled and out of the way," Vince announced, "We should get the girls moving as soon as possible."

"You're really going to take them away?" Mrs. Wolfe sighed. "For how long?"

"For as long as it takes. We have FENRIS agents on the ground and ready to go in Timber Creek. They'll keep you informed with everything that's happening. Ideally, we should move the girls tomorrow."

"I'll take care of that." Evee stood licking the excess blood from the wound on her arm.

"Tomorrow," the word rang in Anna's ears. She should have been afraid, but the warm rush from the bonding ritual ran through her veins, holding the fear at bay.

CHAPTER 13
DRIVE MY CAR

Rain blurred across the windows as the Hornet sped down the highway. Anna watched Timber Creek's landmarks disappear one by one as they made their way out of town. The morning of goodbyes had already been heartbreaking, but watching her world drift away made Anna feel worse.

Today had been chosen for their trip due to the weather. Had it been sunny they would have waited until evening. Apparently she could no longer enjoy direct sunlight without precautions. As implausible as it seemed, Anna wasn't going to put the rule to the test. She found her eyes were more sensitive to light and her skin sometimes itched in its presence. So far she hadn't erupted into a ball of fire when struck with a sunbeam, but she wasn't going to tempt fate.

Anna sat in the back seat with Susan who remained unusually quiet as they left town. The only noise, aside from the rumble of the engine and the rain, was soft music drifting from the stereo.

Les, sitting passenger side, reached up to play with the iPod on the dash.

"Don't even think about it." Evee's lips curled slightly, threatening a snarl even as a human.

"Aw come on!" Les squirmed in his seat. He hadn't stopped fidgeting since the girls were picked up.

"My car, my rules," Evee said, as she drove through the rain. "Music is the driver's choice."

Les twisted himself around to talk to the girls, "Which means nothing past the 80s!"

"What's wrong with the 80s?" Evee said in mock hurt.

"Nothing, but you could stand to mix it up a little more!"

"I like familiar music when I'm driving. It relaxes me."

Anna found the siblings bickering strangely comforting. As if there was nothing to worry about. As if everything in the whole world were normal.

The sound of conversation drew Susan from her staring contest with the car window and she spoke up, "So where's Vince right now? He didn't want to tag along?"

"I don't think road trips are his style," Les tilted his head back.

"But he was fine with us taking one?"

"I thought it best to take you myself." Evee ran her fingers along the wheel, settling her hands into a comfortable position. "I'm sure Vince would have had you transported in an armored car if he could get one, but it's not necessary. Hunter's not going to attack us on the road."

"Why not?" Anna asked, trying to catch a glimpse of Evee's eyes through the rear view mirror.

"Too open," Les said. "Besides, I don't think he'll be ready for round two with your body guard." He playfully cuffed his sister's arm.

Evee shrugged it off, "I have every confidence we'll make it to our destination intact."

"So," Susan stared blankly at the space between Les and Evee, "How'd you guys get involved with this Hunter guy anyway?"

"It's a long story," Evee said in a low, almost threatening tone, a warning not to push the topic.

Susan leaned forward, either oblivious to Evee's signals or not willing to relent, "But there's something I don't get. You guys aren't really FENRIS agents are you? I mean, you're not like those other suits."

The rain beat uncomfortably loud on the windows in the silence that followed. Les opened his mouth to say something, but thought better of it.

Evee grunted in annoyance. "I was an agent a long time ago. Right after my awakening, Hunter murdered someone very dear to me. I got involved with FENRIS then, intent on bringing him to justice, but the years rolled by, and Hunter's attacks were infrequent at best..."

"Evee was a great agent," Les said. "FENRIS wanted her to stay on but..."

"But my heart wasn't in it," Evee cut him off, "I wanted to do something constructive instead of obsessing over something I couldn't resolve."

"Which was when you got the idea to start Red Oaks!" Les grinned.

"Whoa, wait," Susan said, "You made the place we're going to?"

"I was one of the founders, yes." Evee brushed it off as if it were nothing.

"No way! What about Vince? Was he a founder too?"

"No, though he's supported us for many years prior to taking on the job of headmaster."

"Wow! I can't wait to see what it's like!" Susan said. "But does that make you part of FENRIS or part of the school or what?"

"Les and I both play a part at Red Oaks. I retired from FENRIS long ago, but I negotiated that I could come back and consult for any cases that came up regarding Hunter. FENRIS was happy to oblige back then. I don't think they could have seen how long this would take. I'm sure they regret that deal now."

"I doubt it," Les scoffed. "You're the best resource they have at catching him."

"Maybe, but repeated failures take their toll on a person." Evee's eyes finally flicked up to the rear view mirror where they found Anna staring back. Evee looked away.

"You didn't fail this time!" Anna gripped the seat beneath her, forcing her body forward. "I'm alive because of you. You know that right?"

"Are you?" Evee said, her voice distant.

"Anna's right!" Susan leaned in next to her friend, pushing her face through the gap between the passenger and driver's seat. "Maybe he got away, but things could have been much worse! And this time we'll catch him for sure!"

"We?" Les raised an eyebrow at Susan.

"We're a team aren't we? A pack! And I'm not going to let anyone mess with my friends!"

"And who's going to protect us from you?" Les teased.

Susan reeled, but didn't give in, "Hey, I've gotten way better at mastering my shifting!"

"'Mastering' isn't quite the word I would have used," Les said. "Besides you barely know the extent of your Gift! It takes a while to take full advantage of your abilities."

"Then why don't you give us a crash course right now? You've got a captive audience for a few hours."

"Well, you were right about one thing Sue," Les conceded, "Our true power isn't in our individual strengths, but that we're a team. You can't take on the world alone."

"Neither should you and Evee. I know you guys are super powerful and awesome, but this is our fight too!"

"I'm on your side Sue, believe it or not," Evee stuck out an elbow trying to push Susan back into her seat. "We want to include you and Anna. I think that will make all the difference between success or failure. Hunter knows us, especially me, but the one thing he didn't count on was the two of you. I think underestimating you two caused his downfall."

"Not that I did anything special." Anna felt her cheeks grow warm. Being praised was hard enough when she deserved it, but she couldn't fathom how she had any power to change the situation she found herself in a few days ago.

"You survived." Admiration shone in Evee's eyes as they flashed up to the mirror.

"Not through any fault of my own."

"You two should listen to yourselves," Les rolled his eyes. "Two broken records playing the same tune."

The car swerved as Evee swatted at Les. Anna retreated into the car door, her face burning.

"OK! Uncle, I give!" Les cringed, and Evee went back to driving. "Seriously though guys, we've got to stop blaming ourselves for the past and focus on what we can do now."

"That's right! And we can do a lot!" Susan didn't miss the chance to remind Les.

Anna lay her cheek against the cool glass of the window as Susan and Les continued to argue. Their voices began to pound in her ears and the car kept spinning in her vision, so she closed her eyes. The voices in the car drifted in and out, but instead of growing louder, they faded in and out of nothingness.

A hand shook Anna's shoulder, rather rudely. She tried to tell whoever was interrupting her nap to go away, but her mouth refused to form words. She felt heavy, like she was sinking toward the floor.

"Anna, are you..."

"... over Evee!"

"... something's wrong back..."

The car door supporting Anna pulled away and she began to fall, but instead of hitting the ground, Anna fell into something soft and the smell of the white wolf enveloped her. She must be dreaming again.

The smell of blood cut through the air like a knife, and Anna's eyes flashed open. Her stomach growled like an animal at the sight of the beautiful line of crimson running down an arm. Everything else faded from importance. She grabbed the arm, bringing the wound to her lips, lapping at the generously flowing blood. It tasted heavenly, pumping hot and fresh from a warm body. Anna buried her face in the arm, licking greedily.

As her thirst slaked, the world around her came into focus again. A drop of rain hit her face and Anna realized she was on a roadside in the middle of nowhere with rain sprinkling down on her. Evee hunched over her, shielding her from the rain, and the chill and damp began to register in Anna's senses. Evee shifted the arm she had wrapped around Anna's shoulders and Anna realized she was being held upright. She tried to straighten herself, but that only brought her closer to Evee's face and her beautiful blue eyes. Anna thought she might swoon again.

"Are you alright?" Evee's face hovered inches above hers. She could feel Evee's warm breath ghosting over her face.

Anna felt incredibly warm despite the weather. She tried to string together a response, but the delicious smell of blood still hung in the air. Looking towards its source, she finally connected the bleeding arm with the woman holding her, sheltering her from the rain. "Oh my God! What have I done?"

"When was the last time you ate?" Evee asked.

"This morning! I swear!"

"And did you eat all of it?"

"Um... maybe..." Anna still wasn't used to her new diet.

Evee sighed, letting her shoulders hunch over even further. Rain trickled past her protective posture. "We should probably increase your feedings until your body gets used to things. Turning is a lot to recover from. Do you need more?"

Anna recoiled from the offered arm, red smeared across the pale skin. "Oh Evee, I'm so sorry! Doesn't it hurt?"

Evee's lips twitched into a grin, "I've been through worse." She hesitated, averting her eyes, "We have blood in the cooler too, if Les ever finds it, if you'd prefer..."

Anna drew Evee's arm to her lips, gently running her tongue over the wounds, cleaning them. Anna almost lost herself again in the sweet scent of Evee's blood, but remembered the gracious person the blood came from. She didn't want to hurt Evee any more than she already had. It took every ounce of will for Anna to draw back from the arm, and get to her feet. Her legs wobbled beneath her, but she still rose. "Thank you Evee. I'm so sorry about this."

"It's not your fault, I should have been monitoring your condition better." Evee went to stand, but faltered, leaning against the car. She cursed under her breath, holding a fist above the roof of the car as if holding back from slamming it into the metal.

Gravel crunched as Les ran up to them. Anna saw that he and Susan had been standing off a bit down the road. Susan flashed her a knowing smile and Anna wanted to crawl into a hole and disappear.

"Argh!" Evee's growl cut through Anna's thoughts. "Easy with that stuff will you?"

Les was already at work, cleaning and binding Evee's arm. "You know we have blood in the cooler right?"

Evee winced, "Maybe if you'd found it quicker I wouldn't have had to open up my own arm... again."

"It's not my fault the trunk is loaded with junk! Well, no harm, no foul." Les tied a bandage around the wound, before turning to inspect Anna. He ran his fingers over Anna's wrist, and checked her eyes. "You'll be alright. But you," Les pointed at Evee, "Shouldn't be driving right now."

"You're not driving my baby!" Evee tried to stand tall, but wavered when she let go of the side of the car.

"Don't make me pull 'Doctor's orders' on you. You've lost a lot of blood and it'll take time for your body to regenerate. You need to rest."

Evee stared at Les for a long moment before dropping her eyes to the ground. "Fine." She skulked over to the passenger side of the car and everyone took that as their cue to get in.

"That's the spirit! Sit back and enjoy the ride!" Les gloated over his victory.

"Not with you driving." Evee plopped herself in the seat as Les hopped in behind the wheel. Susan and Anna crawled into the back, quiet as they watched the siblings hash things out.

"Oh but it gets better!" Les flipped through the music selection before blasting the speakers, "It's time for Britney bitch!"

Evee's complexion turned an unhealthy shade. "I. Hate. You."

CHAPTER 14
HOME SWEET HOME

It was dark by the time the Hornet pulled off the highway, traveling down more isolated roads. Darkness swallowed the car, leaving only a streak of pavement illuminated by the headlights along with the soft glow of the dash. The rain had stopped and the world was still, holding its breath, waiting for something to happen.

Anna had been quiet after her fainting spell, content to listen to the others in the car talk amongst themselves. But as darkness fell, even Les and Susan stopped talking, turning to their windows or their thoughts. There wasn't much to look at through the windows. The sky was still cloudy and trees blocked out what little light might have reached them from the city. If she focused, Anna could make out the branches as they drove by; a new world emerging from the shadows. Anna shook her head turning away. It was disconcerting, not only how well she could see in the dark, but how much her body enjoyed the lack of light.

Les turned off down a side road and Evee sat up alert. The darkness faded slowly into soft light, illuminating a gate. The iron doors were drawn back, waiting for them to pass. After driving through, the metal clanged shut behind them. Anna didn't see anyone at the gate, but the hairs on the back of her neck standing on end told her otherwise. She could feel the eyes of FENRIS agents on them, even though she couldn't spot them through the trees.

Lampposts, alternating along the edge of the drive, kept the path lit with a yellow glow. Then the trees drew away, revealing a stately lawn, leading to a towering, castle-like building made of stone, its spires and roofs reaching toward the sky. Everything was well lit, dispelling any shadows that might have crept too close.

Les veered off down a side lane, pulling around to the side of the building instead of bringing them to the front entrance. A puddle of fluorescent light spilled out from an open garage wedged in the building's foundation. Les parked inside between a disassembled motorcycle and and another car covered in a tarp, parked right up against the wall to conserve as much space as possible. The garage was a mess of tools and parts, smelling of grease.

Les cut the engine. "Welcome home."

"Not much has changed." Evee opened her door. "Jessie still hasn't cleaned up his mess."

The name rung a bell in Anna's heart, but before she could ask, Vince stepped out from a door leading inside the building. Amusement crossed his face as he glanced between Evee and Les, "You let *him* drive?"

"Don't rub it in." Evee slammed the door behind her.

"Yeah, she's pretty short in the temper department today," Les got out and moved around to the back of the car, opening the trunk and emptying its contents on the garage floor as Susan and Anna got out of the back seat.

"Trouble along the way?" Vince asked.

"No." Evee straightened. "Just a long trip and we're tired is all."

Vince raised an eyebrow, "Very well, I've come to collect the girls and show them to their dorm."

Evee's shoulders slumped. "You're going to separate us?"

"What did you think sis? We were all going to gather around the fire in your *closet* and cuddle?"

"It's a *study*, and it's not that small!" Evee raised a hand to her temple digging her fingers hard into her skull. "I don't know what I thought, but I don't like being separated right now."

"We'll be fine!" Susan radiated a confidence Anna didn't feel.

"Everything is arranged, including the security," Vince reassured her. "If you like, we can look into alternative arrangements in the morning, but I think the girls will be quite comfortable where I've set them up."

Evee sighed and nodded her assent, too tired to argue.

"Excellent. Girls, if you would follow me." Vince held the door open for them.

Anna grabbed her bags from the garage floor, her heart jumping into her throat.

"We'll see you for breakfast in the morning!" Les patted her shoulder, waving them toward the door. "Bright and early!"

Anna cringed at the word 'bright,' but managed to wave goodnight to Les. She raised her hand to wave goodnight to Evee, but faltered, tripping over the steps out of the garage. "Good night!" she squeaked out before running to catch up with Vince and Susan.

Vince led them through a series of halls winding their way through the building. The walls were covered with wood panels and the doors decorated with ornate carved posts. Light from wall sconces wove upward giving the halls a warm glow. It was beautiful, smelling of rich wood. Vince's shoes clacked along the floor, and the echos disappeared through the maze of halls. Voices whispered from behind closed doors making the building feel alive and full of secrets.

Vince brought them to a door that led outside to a covered walkway. Gargoyles leered from their perches on stone pillars, holding up the roof or carrying lanterns in their teeth. Anna wanted to stop and examine them, but Susan had already run down the walkway to another door to escape the winter chill. Once in the warmth of the new building, Vince addressed them in a quiet voice.

"Welcome to Falconer House! This is one of our oldest dorms, but I think you'll find it pleasant. Obviously you're not the only ones in residence so we ask you to be courteous and think of our other students while you're here. Keep noise to a minimum and things should be fine."

They made their way up the stairs to the third floor, right down to the last door at the end of the hall. Vince took a key from his pocket and let them inside.

"Wow, they don't make them like they used to!" Susan marveled at the spacious room. "I think the closet in here is bigger than most university dorm rooms!"

The room was long, a sloped ceiling revealing the roof line with a single dormer window dividing the room in half. Each side had its own bed, desk, dresser and – as Susan had noted – closet. Dark wood paneling ran around the lower half of the walls contrasting with the light grey plaster of the upper half. Anna felt suddenly small standing in the room, clutching her bags. The room was cold and empty.

"I'm glad you like it," Vince handed a key to each girl. "The bathroom is down the hall and if you need anything, knock on the door across from you. FENRIS agents will be stationed there at all times."

Anna didn't like the idea of going to strangers for help. "Where's Evee and Les?"

"They have their own quarters in the main building. If you're uncomfortable here we can work out new arrangements tomorrow."

"No way! This is so cool!" Susan dumped her bags at the foot of a bed, flopping backwards onto the mattress. "We're good for now. Thanks Vince!"

"Alright. I'll be by to pick you up tomorrow morning. Have a good night."

After Vince's footsteps faded away down the hall Susan perked up. "Isn't this awesome!"

"Yeah. Great." Anna couldn't shake the fear her new surroundings brought up. She sat on the edge of her bed and studied the grain of the wood floor.

"Sorry, I know this is kind of scary."

"Kind of?!" Anna squealed before clapping a hand over her mouth as she remembered Vince's warning about noise.

"Relax Anna! We can talk, we just have to keep it down. And yeah, you're right, it is scary."

"You don't have a psychopath trying to kill you!" Anna couldn't keep the panic out of her voice. Scary was an understatement. Try terrifying.

"You're right." Susan got up folding her arms across her chest, her confidence melting away. "Look, I'm scared too but I'm not going to lose you, no matter what."

"I'm glad I'm not in this alone." Anna smiled at her. "It feels so empty here, so lonely."

"It's only strange because it's new." Susan waved the thought away.

"I've never been away from home before." Anna's throat tightened. "I miss my mom and I'm scared." She pulled her legs up to her chest, curling herself tight in a ball, holding herself together.

Susan sat down next to her, putting an arm around Anna's shoulders. "It's going to be alright. You have me. You have Les and Evee and a whole platoon of FENRIS agents to protect you. It'll work out."

"I hope so." Anna leaned into Susan. Her friend's familiar scent was comforting. "I'm glad you're here, and..." Anna bit her lip finding the strength to say what had been on her mind, "And I'm glad you're not treating me any different, now that... you know."

"That you're a vampire?" Susan looked serious for a second, but couldn't keep her face straight for long. "Sorry, I couldn't resist."

"Your teasing is *so* comforting."

"So is your sarcasm. Seriously though, it doesn't matter to me. Gay, straight, vampire, mermaid... Did you think things would be different between us?"

"I was afraid they would be, yes. You have no idea how many fears crossed my mind."

"That's the danger of being in your head so much! I'm glad you told me though. I want you to feel comfortable telling me stuff, no matter what. I've dumped a lot of junk on you lately, so if you want to vent about something, vent!"

Anna drew a blank. Now that she no longer had to censor herself, nothing came to mind. "If I think of anything I'll let you know."

"Aw common! There's gotta be something on your mind."

"I think there's too many things on my mind. That's the problem." Anna would have left it at that, but Susan sat still, waiting patiently for her to open up. "Everything's so new and scary. I'm in a place I've never been, surrounded by people I don't know, waiting for something bad to happen. If I'm not a nervous wreck now, I will be soon."

"Well, you've got me. Not to mention Les and Evee."

"Les is fine," The memory of his essence was soothing. "He's like a brother."

"Cuz I need another one of those like a hole in the head." Susan laughed. "But I like him too. What about Evee?"

Icy blue eyes filled Anna's mind. "She seems so cold... and yet, she's not. I think she's a really warm person inside."

"Uh huh." Susan drew out the last word, a stupid smirk crawling up her face.

"What?" Anna pulled back, afraid she had said something revealing.

"Nothing, you just got this dreamy look on your face

when you started talking about her."

"I did not!"

"You don't have to deny it, you know. It's cool. She's pretty hot."

"She's also like a hundred years older than me!"

"So you've thought about this?" Susan leaned in, not letting Anna off the hook.

"Sue..." Anna was only going to warn her once.

Susan drew back, shrugging, "You can keep denying it, but the only person you're fooling is yourself."

Anna slumped forward. Instinct told her to hide and deny any feelings she had, especially in such a complicated situation. She was terrified of opening the Pandora's box that was her heart. "She saved my life. I don't remember much of her from when I... when I turned, but this afternoon in the car!" Anna held her burning cheeks in her cool hands, "She's always so gruff on the outside, but the way she looked at me when she was holding me, the way she offered her arm to me... She's really a big softy on the inside. I can tell."

"Wow... you got it bad!"

"Shut up!" Anna shoved Susan off the bed.

"Hey! No roughhousing in the dormitories!" Susan scolded her, doing her best Vince impression.

Anna clamped a hand over her mouth to stifle her laughter. "You seem to be in pretty good spirits, considering your problems haven't gone away."

Susan shrugged, looking more serious, "It's not that I've forgotten, but there's comfort in knowing that it's going to be addressed. I don't know what's going to happen with me yet but Les has talked to me about it. He seems confident I'll be held accountable somehow, but not in a lock me away type of solution. I don't know. I haven't been thinking about it much since your problem became the bigger one."

"My problem is more immediate, but I think both our problems are big. Let's not compete in that department."

"I think we'd both lose if that were the case."

"Right." Anna stood beside Susan taking her hand in hers. "Let's get through this together. One step at a time."

CHAPTER 15
DAY BREAKS

Anna became aware of the shift in light. She ducked her head under the covers but was unable to escape dawn's approaching glow. It penetrated the curtains and filled up the room to the point where Anna could no longer ignore it. She was awake. She could hear Susan's even breathing across the room. Anna envied the fact that her friend was still asleep, but still didn't want to wake her.

Anna drew back the covers, placing her feet on the floor. She felt out the creaks and groans of the wood as she pulled on fresh clothes. Making it to the door proved more difficult and the floor boards creaked mercilessly under her. She froze, hoping Susan wouldn't notice. The other girl lay still as a stone. Anna scolded herself for worrying so much. She left the room, silent as a shadow, closing the door behind her, with only the soft click of the latch catching the plate.

The fluorescent bulbs in the hall glared their obnoxious flickering light. Anna wasn't sure what was worse, those lights or the sun. Anna squinted against their bluish tint, willing her eyes to adjust faster. A noise from the room across the hall startled her. Anna nearly jumped out of her skin, but instead, she landed a good four feet away from her spot before the door. She marveled at the distance. Her muscles had gotten stronger, her reflexes sharper.

Another shuffling noise from the FENRIS room and Anna reacted by bolting down the hall. When she reached the stairwell a thought came to her and she grabbed the railing, throwing herself over the banister, landing on the next platform down. She stared at her legs, amazed they could take a jump from that height without any damage, nor even much effort at all. She waited in the stairwell a moment, listening for sounds of pursuit, but it was quiet.

Anna let go the breath she had been holding and wandered down the rest of the stairs. She paused at the outside door, but pushed it open and headed out into the covered archway. The sky was lightening, casting lavender shadows across the snow that had fallen during the night. The brightness, even in the predawn, hurt her eyes, so she jogged down the archway to the safety of the great building in front of her.

It was warm inside, the lighting soft and the smells comforting. Anna wondered how old the building was. It seemed to hold an age's worth of memory in its walls. She wandered the corridors with no particular destination in mind. She shouldn't have been wandering at all, but the light in the dorm was uncomfortable and she couldn't sleep. She needed something familiar to comfort her and recalled Vince saying that Les and Evee were staying in this building. However, now that she was here, she had no idea where to find them.

The hall exited into an expansive foyer. Its ceiling vaulted three storeys above her, the stairs and gallery on the second floor opening into the room, edged by a stone railing. Two giant doors faced the outside and Anna realized she stood in the building's main entrance. The marble floor at her feet was made of an intricate inlay, displaying the school's crest, an oak tree on a shield. Anna walked along the Latin inscription that encircled the emblem.

"It says, 'As an oak through the ages.'"

Anna startled as Vince's voice rang through the empty hall. Searching for its source, Anna's heart fell when she realized Vince was approaching her from the way she had come. "Were you following me the whole time?"

"Not at all. I announced myself on my arrival." He joined her at the foot of the inlay, examining it with her. "Though I did get a call from FENRIS telling me you'd left your room. I figured you might want to explore a bit on your own."

"Am I allowed to do that?"

"I'd like to think that within these walls all my pupils are safe. Of course I've never run into a situation like yours before. I think we'll find out today what FENRIS expects of us. There will be a meeting this afternoon."

Anna traced the pattern of the inlay with her toe.

"Did you sleep well?" Vince insisted on engaging her in conversation.

"Things started out fine. I woke up early once it started to get light out, then I couldn't get back to sleep." The sun was now peeking over the horizon, shedding its first rays of light through the hall's windows, irritating Anna. "How do you stand it?"

Vince chuckled, "I've had many years of practice. My duties as headmaster mean I must be available during the daylight hours."

"It's so tempting to become nocturnal."

"You'll get used to the light sensitivity over time, among other things."

"Like breakfast?"

"Yes. Why don't I show you around the kitchens? It's still early, but that means we'll beat the rush."

"I'd hate to get between a bunch of hungry werewolves and their breakfast!" Anna followed Vince through the building.

It was an impressive maze of lecture halls, classrooms and studies. The second floor even housed an extensive library.

Vince was in his element as tour guide, "There are other buildings too. Our dorms and athletic center along with the labs and medical center."

"It's like your own private village!"

"Yes, we like to think we're self-sustaining. Oh and the grounds! Ah..." A shadow fell across Vince's face, "My apologies. I can't imagine FENRIS letting you out on the grounds, but we have acres upon acres covered in trails! When this whole fiasco blows over, I'm sure you'll enjoy them."

Anna appreciated Vince's optimism. Her frayed nerves could use more comfort.

As they drew closer to the kitchens the smell of food and the noise from the dining hall increased. Anna had to blink hard against the morning light streaming through the East facing windows of the dinning hall. The bright light coupled with the din and smell of food made Anna nauseous. She raised a hand to shield her eyes.

"Take deep breaths," Vince said. "Don't let it overwhelm you. You can adjust to this."

Anna did as she was told and focused on her breath. Eventually, the noise subsided and her head stopped swimming, but it was still hard to open her eyes to such bright light. Instead she let her gaze wander to where the shadows in the room lay. Four long tables ran lengthwise down the room away from were they stood. At the end was a dais with another long table set perpendicular to the rest. At the raised table, covered in the shadowed side, sat Evee in the form Anna had first seen her, somewhere between wolf and human. The morning light highlighted the edge of her white fur, and she wore a loose teal sweater that complimented her eyes.

Vince led Anna through the throng of tables and she noticed a good number of diners turn to stare at her before going back to their conversations, their voices too low for her to hear. She wanted to crawl into a corner, not sit on a dais while everyone could stare at her.

They approached Evee who didn't look up from her morning tea and newspaper, "Did you sleep alright?"

"Um... I... I suppose. As alright as sleep gets." Anna stumbled over her words, feeling eyes on her from around the hall.

Vince pulled a chair out for Anna. She sat down curling away from prying eyes.

"You ladies sit tight, while I fetch something for Anna and myself." Before Anna could protest, Vince was gone.

Evee set her cup on its saucer and finally looked up at Anna. "Taking a tour of the grounds I see?"

"N... no, I mean, I was just walking back from where we had gone last night. I didn't think..." Anna balled her hands into fists in her lap, her knuckles turning white. "I... I wasn't thinking at all. I should have waited for someone to come, or woken Sue or a FENRIS agent or something, but I couldn't bring myself to do it. I wanted to be alone for a bit."

"It's alright Anna, you didn't do anything wrong," Evee's eyes crinkled with sympathy. "But you're right, you shouldn't be going off whenever you feel like it without someone with you."

Anna groaned. Being around others twenty four seven was exhausting.

"Listen, why don't you come by my study when you need a break? It's small and I can't guarantee I won't be working there myself, but..."

Anna's heart leapt. "That sounds great!"

"If you ever need to get away, you're more than welcome to use it. I'll have to find my spare key."

Anna opened her mouth to express her gratitude but was interrupted by a chair scrapping beside her. Susan plunked herself on the seat, glaring at Anna through her disheveled mane, "Where were you?"

"Uh..."

"It's a good thing Les came to wake me up," Susan yawned, stretching her arms out, "And that he told me you'd already gone down to breakfast!"

"I wouldn't worry," Anna said, "Everyone seems to be keeping tabs on me just fine."

Les pulled out a chair next to Evee. "Well, it's sort of our job you know."

Anna wasn't sure if he was joking or if they really were following her every move.

"Anyway, Sue and I are going to grab a plate. The other two should be along any minute." Les got up and sauntered over to the cafeteria with Susan.

"Other two?" Anna felt the strange tingling she had before in the garage.

"You'll meet your other pack brothers soon." Evee sipped her tea.

Anna traced circles on the table, wondering what her other pack mates were like but too afraid to ask. Sue and Les returned with heaping plates and two other people in tow. Anna felt her skin prickle at the sight of them and knew these were the 'brothers' Evee spoke of. The first one was a boy who looked no older than Anna, but she remembered appearance might not be a true indicator of his age. Looks among werewolves were deceiving. He was tall and thin with long blond hair tied back in a loose pony tail. The other man looked older, around Evee's age. His hair was short, his skin dark and his eyes curious. Anna guessed he was older than he appeared.

Les placed a mug in front of Anna, "Vince sends his regards. Unfortunately, he's been called away, but he wanted to make sure you were eating properly."

The enticing scent of blood floated up from the mug as Anna curled her fingers around it. It warmed her hands. She didn't realize how hungry she was until fresh blood was put in front of her. As much as she wanted to bury her face in the mug, Anna hesitated watching her pack seat themselves around her.

Evee straightened in her seat, puffing out her chest. "Girls, this is Sam," she gestured to the older man with dark skin, "And this is Jessie." The boy with the long hair nodded. "And our newest arrivals, Susan and Anna."

There was a curious moment where everyone stared at each other, but it wasn't uncomfortable. It felt like coming home to a family dinner where Anna hadn't seen her relatives in a long while.

"Well you can all tuck in when you're ready," Evee reached over and grabbed a piece of toast from Les' plate, taking a large bite.

"Hey!"

Everyone moved all at once, the spell binding them broken. Forks scraped plates, tongues wagged, and copious amounts of food were inhaled by the werewolves. Anna looked down at her mug, painfully aware of the difference between her and the others.

"Eat." Les commanded from across the table.

"What?" Anna pulled herself from her thoughts.

"Just eat," Les said in a softer voice. "It's nothing we haven't seen before."

Anna raised the mug to her lips. The blood was still fresh, sliding down her throat to warm her belly. Like a cat lapping at cream, Anna was embarrassed at how much she enjoyed the sensation. She forced the mug down to the table in order to turn her attention back to the conversation at hand. She relaxed when she saw that no one was staring at her or acting like she was doing something weird. The conversation went on as if everything were normal. The meal took a leisurely pace and everyone lingered at the table long after plates had been scraped clean.

Evee's ears perked forward and she stared at something over Anna's shoulder. "I'm glad to see you all getting along, but I'm afraid I have to break things up."

"Good morning everyone!" A pudgy, older man with a bushy mustache approached waving at them.

"Thanks for coming Walter." Evee smiled, but it didn't reach her eyes.

"What's going on?" Anna didn't like the sudden gloom hovering over the table.

Walter faced Anna, "I'm here to give you a little tour of the grounds!"

Something clicked in Anna's mind, "Just me? What about everyone else?"

Evee stood, "I'm taking everyone who can transform out for a run. We need to stretch our legs."

"That's not fair!" Susan jumped to her feet nearly knocking her chair over.

"No one said it was fair." Evee's ears flattened back against her skull. "But we can't take Anna around the grounds with us. It's too dangerous."

"But not for me?" Susan crossed her arms over her chest, staring defiantly at Evee.

"Go." Anna forced herself to sound more confident than she felt. "It's fine, I understand."

Susan looked back and forth between Anna and Evee before letting her eyes drop to the table. "Fine."

"Don't worry, we won't be long," Les rose and began gathering the plates. "It's important for you to get a better grip on your transformations Sue, not to mention dealing with the Wolf inside. Besides, it'll be too sunny for Anna to go outside."

Susan didn't move.

"Go!"Anna insisted. "At least one of us can go out and have some fun!"

"I don't want to leave you," Susan said.

"I'll be fine. I promise."

"If you say so."

"Good." Evee nodded at the boys, "We'll meet you out at the shack shortly."

Les, Jessie and Sam left the table, while Evee took Walter aside for a moment.

Susan tapped at the leg of her chair with her foot. "This sucks."

"It won't be like this forever. We need to be patient right now," Anna said.

"You heard Les! Even if it was safe, they might not let you go out because of the sun. It's like a werewolves only club or something."

"I've been through worse."

Susan finally let herself grin at Anna, "Try not to get into too much trouble while I'm gone."

"Don't worry, I won't get into trouble unless you're around to blame it on."

CHAPTER 16
THE PACK

The sunlight reflecting off the snow blinded Susan. She blinked the spots in her eyes away as her vision adjusted. It was cold out, but pleasant with the sun warming her face. The grounds were quiet save for the crunching of their footsteps on the snow. Susan followed Evee away from the buildings, toward the edge of the lawn. A squat log cabin sat at the treeline, sheltered by overhanging branches. Susan guessed this was what the pack had referred to lovingly as "the shack." Chickadees squawked at their approach and the scent of pine filled the air.

Evee pushed the door open and Susan noticed it was made to swing in either direction. The building was split in two sections. The main area was a change room. Alcoves lined the walls, each with their own series of hooks and shelves for clothing. A wall of shelves ran down the middle, separating the room into two aisles. The other side of the building revealed an open row of showers. Susan could hear the boys on the other side of the shelves. The layout of the change area felt a little too open to be comfortable.

While Susan was taking everything in, Evee had already started to remove her clothes. "Pick a spot and remember your number." She tapped a little brass plate screwed to the shelf in front of her.

Susan chose an alcove a few steps away from Evee's and began unlacing her boots. "We all change in one big room?"

"When you see your pack mates naked enough times, it stops being an issue, but the boys have been kind enough to give us our own row for now."

"And the showers?"

"First come first served, though we shouldn't be getting too dirty today due to the snow. You can always go back to your dorm if you want to shower in private."

"It's OK," Susan didn't want to make things more complicated than necessary, but she couldn't shake the uneasy thought of seeing a bunch of guys naked in an open shower.

"Don't worry. The boys will keep to themselves until you feel comfortable. We don't want to scare you!"

"We're not scary!" Les shouted over the shelves.

"Shouldn't you be outside by now?" Evee growled.

"Already there!" The sound of nails clicking, ran across tile and a draft swooshed through the building as another door at the back pushed open.

"Do you guys always tease each other?" Susan hardly saw them behave otherwise.

"Les likes to push limits." Evee didn't sound impressed. "Don't you have a little brother? You must know what it's like."

"Sort of," Susan chewed her lip thinking about her family. "Ben's not that good with comebacks though, and I think my mom would pitch a fit if I were to tease him all the time."

"Oh, he'll find his stride one day, and then you'll never hear the end of it, whether your mother is around or not." Evee bowed to the ground, shifting smoothly to all fours. Sitting back on her haunches she waited for Susan to do the same.

Susan took a moment to gather her bearings before shifting, the cold air prickling goosebumps on her skin. Her body shuddered, jerking her arms forward, she landed on them much less gracefully than Evee. At least she landed on her paws and not her face.

Evee strolled around the corner and Susan followed. Another swinging door came into view and Evee butted her head against it, opening it to the bright snow covered wilderness beyond. A broad path lead down from the back of the shack into the bush. Ahead lay a clearing where the snow was packed down in the center, a hub of many crisscrossing trails that met before shooting off in different directions through the trees.

Evee sniffed the edges of the trails while the boys played in the clearing. Les ran around harassing a much larger grey wolf and funny looking black and brown canine that Susan recognized as an African wild dog. Susan knew by smell that the wolf was Jessie. He nipped at Les' ears, but didn't seem interested in playing. When he saw Susan however, Jessie lowered his head and moved towards her. Susan shrank back from the intimidating wolf. After a preliminary sniff, Jessie appeared as uninterested with her as he was with Les.

Sam pounced on Les grabbing him by the scruff of his neck, wrestling him to the ground. Les whimpered his defeat but bounced up as soon as Sam let go. Les hurtled over to Susan with Sam at his heels. They both sniffed at Susan, wagging their tails and bowing, inviting her to play.

Evee shifted into her hybrid form, towering over the pack. Everyone snapped to attention. "Alright, we're not going far, and we're staying on the trails. Stick together and remember we're getting Susan used to her legs. Feel free to mark. Hunter will know we're here and the girls aren't alone."

"Do you think that's a good idea?" Les shifted so he could talk, but lay down in the snow instead of getting up to Evee's height.

"I don't think it'll hurt us to frustrate him a bit." Evee's lips drew back as she bore her teeth to her brother.

Les shrugged and shifted back to a coyote, shaking the snow from his coat as he stood.

Evee leapt forward shifting and landing on her paws. The others followed her lead and Susan bounded after them.

Running in a pack was strange, but Susan began to pick up on the ebb and flow of her pack's body language. Words weren't needed. In fact, the more Susan relaxed, the more in tune she felt with everyone around her. Relaxing also helped her get the feel of her own wolf body. The less she worried about it, the easier it was to control. Susan had to trust the beast inside, not fight it, which was difficult. No matter how much Susan opened up, there was always a small nagging doubt in the back of her brain. *What if I can't control it? What if I hurt someone again?* Susan shoved her fears aside. The sooner she got a grip on being a werewolf, the better.

Les bumped into her shoulder, causing Susan to stumble. He nipped at her heels before dancing out of teeth's reach, his lips drawn back in a canine grin. Susan went to bump him back, aiming for his shoulder but misjudged the distance and tripped face first into a snow drift. Susan freed herself, shaking the snow from her fur. The pack doubled back, circling around her until she got to her feet again and then they were off as if nothing had happened.

The pack galloped down trails, exploring nooks and crannies along the way. Occasionally, Evee would stop, lifting her nose to the air and everyone would become silent, ears swiveling trying to catch some sound Susan remained oblivious to. Then Evee would start and they would be off running again.

It felt great to be able to run. The tension from the previous days melted away as Susan trotted along. Her problems became distant and not altogether real anymore, as Susan lost herself to the physical sensation of running.

All too soon they were standing in the clearing behind the shack again, Susan's legs shuddering underneath her from exertion. Evee watched wordlessly as each pack member entered the building, counting them off one by one. Susan was the last to leave the trails. She didn't want to face whatever problems her human self had to deal with. She slunk past Evee, her head low until it butted against the door of the shack.

Susan shifted easily back into her human self, despite being tired. Evee walked over to her alcove, shifting and reaching for her clothes in one fluid motion.

"You don't even think about it do you?" Susan said in awe.

Evee tugged a shirt over her head before responding, "It's easier if you don't think about it too much. You'll get the hang of it." Her eyes lit up, "So what did you think about your first pack run?"

"Awesome! I want to go again!"

Evee laughed, the stern lines on her face lifting momentarily. "Hopefully we can go again soon, but I'm not holding my breath. I have to go to a meeting now, and I have a feeling FENRIS is going to slap more restrictions on us."

Susan paused, admiring Evee's cunning. "Did you take us out before they told you not to?"

"Something like that. Don't tell me you aren't grateful for a chance to stretch your legs!"

"It's not that," Guilt clawed at Susan's stomach. "Do you really think it was a good idea to go out given everything that's going on?"

"Do you trust me Sue?"

"I want to..."

"Fair enough. In the middle of the day with an entire pack around you, there's no way Hunter posed any kind of threat, and Anna is safe at the school surrounded by FENRIS." Evee brushed her hair behind a pink ear, "Of course if I'm being totally honest with you, I'm hoping that taunting Hunter like this will make him angry, which will make him do something stupid so he's easier to catch. It's a small risk with a big potential payout. I don't know what FENRIS will think, so I acted before they could tell me not to. It all depends who's in charge of the case."

"I thought Walter was?" Susan said confused.

"They're changing things around." Evee didn't sound pleased. "That's what our meeting this afternoon is supposed to be about. Don't worry though, I'll be sure to protect your best interests." Evee grabbed her watch from the shelf and swore under her breath. "That took longer than I thought. I have to go. The boys will escort you back."

"No problem I'll be out in a minute!" Susan said through the shirt covering half her face. As she finished dressing, her thoughts kept circling back to Will. It was hard to reconcile him as the deadly Hunter that had half the werewolf community up in arms. A killer didn't mix with the sweet guy she thought she knew. Then again, maybe everyone had a killer inside them, only some people let it run loose. Susan shuddered as she pulled on her coat.

The swoosh of the door opening made Susan jump. Images of Will and Jim flooded her head and her heart hammered in her chest.

"You coming?" Les's voice echoed through the room. Susan rushed to the door, but when Les saw her, the grin dropped from his face. "What's up?"

"Nothing." Susan forced a smile. She didn't want to recall any more images or feelings. "Let's go."

Les said nothing as he walked by her side toward the school. Jessie and Sam were waiting for them on the path. They took their time walking back and Susan's mood lightened. It was hard to feel down with her pack brothers around.

Les jumped in front of the group, stopping them in their tracks. "I have some paperwork that I've been meaning to catch up on, do you think you three will be alright on your own?"

"Sure." Susan felt safe enough. They were already close to

the school, standing in a blindingly sunny field.

"Why not?" Sam came up behind her. "It'll give us some time to get to know each other."

"That's the plan!" Les said. "You know where to find me if you need me." He walked off toward the school, leaving Susan standing alone with Jessie and Sam.

Susan felt weird being alone with them. Not because she didn't know them, but because they had just met and felt so familiar. It was odd.

"Wanna go for a walk?" Jessie pointed toward a shoveled path lined with trees.

"Can we stay outside?" Susan looked across the open field, waiting for something to jump out at her.

"Pfft," Jessie waved off her concern, "We're practically right next to the school. I can smell FENRIS agents from here!"

"You can?" Susan did a double take over her shoulder. She didn't see anyone and the grounds were eerily quiet.

"I'm surprised you noticed," Sam elbowed Jessie, hiding a smile behind his hand.

"Oh come on! I'm not that spaced out!"

"Are we really being watched?" Susan eyed the boys suspiciously. Maybe they were teasing her.

Sam put a hand on Susan's shoulder. "Close your eyes and focus on your breath."

Susan did as she was told. She could smell Sam and Jessie beside her among the trees and snow. It took a minute, but eventually she caught an unfamiliar scent on the air. She opened her eyes and snapped her head around to where she thought the scent was coming from, but saw nothing.

"Close, but not quite." Sam pointed a little further from where Susan was staring. A man in black with an ear piece stood in the shadow of a doorway. Susan was surprised she had missed him, and a little embarrassed.

"It comes with practice." Sam reassured her, stirring that uncanny feeling of familiarity.

"You guys coming or not?" Jessie was already several feet ahead. As they walked Jessie stopped at the foot of a tree then jumped up – far higher than Susan thought possible – grabbed a branch and pulled himself up on top of it.

"Sometimes I think he should have been a were-monkey." Sam joked.

"Are you two waiting for an invitation?" Jessie swung himself into a fork in the trunk, leaning into it.

"Ladies first." Sam held out his hand toward the tree.

"I don't know if I can jump that high." Susan calculated the distance to the branch Jessie caught. It didn't look like something she could reach.

"Have you tried?"

Susan gritted her teeth, crouched and aimed for the branch. She pushed off with all her strength but instead of falling short, she overshot her target, the branch catching her in the stomach. Then she started slipping backward. Susan scrambled, locking her arms around the branch.

"How's the air up there?" Sam called from the ground.

"Fine!" Susan wheezed.

The branch bent under Jessie's weight as he stepped over to Susan, pulling her up by her coat. The ground beneath her lurched and her balance failed. "I'm going to fall!"

"You won't!" Jessie dragged her to her feet. "Besides, it's not far enough to hurt you."

Susan steadied herself, trying the find her balance on the sagging branch. "How high would I have to be for it to hurt?"

"Depends how you land I think. Our bodies can take a lot of punishment. More than any human's." Jessie called down to Sam. "Hey old man, you coming up?"

"I don't think so, I like having two feet firmly planted on the ground!"

"Suit yourself." Jessie climbed back over to the fork, leaning his back against the trunk. Reaching in his pocket he pulled out a lighter and cigarette. "Sam knows what I'm up to. He probably doesn't want to reek like a cigarette. You smoke?"

"No."

"Good. They're bad for you." Jessie held the cigarette in his lips, cupping one hand over the end and sparking the lighter with the other.

The burning tobacco smelled acrid and foul to Susan. She didn't want to offend Jessie, but couldn't help the sneer curling up her lip. "I didn't realize you smoked."

"I haven't in a long time, but old habits die hard." Jessie took a long drag, and his face relaxed. "This whole thing with Hunter has got me freaking out... sorry, you probably feel worse than I do."

"I try not to think about it too much." Susan crouched, lowering herself onto what she hoped would be a comfortable branch. "I wish it was over and done with, so I could go home."

"But then you wouldn't get to hang out with us!"

Susan was starting to like Jessie, but she wished they had met under different circumstances. "As much fun as this is, I miss my family. I miss school. I miss having a normal life."

"You might never get that back." Jessie puffed a smoky laugh through his lips.

"I know, but I feel all cooped up here. I can't go anywhere by myself and everyone is on edge."

"It sucks. I wish things were different too. We must be giving you a bad first impression."

"Speak for yourself!" Sam yelled from below.

Jessie snorted, not dignifying Sam with a response.

Susan changed the subject. "So where are you from?"

"Ohio."

Susan struggled to make a connection, "How'd you end up here?"

Jessie's gaze grew distant. "Funny story that one. It's all Sam's fault really."

"Don't blame me for your choices!"

"Did I really have a choice?" Jessie said, before a shadow fell across his face. "No, you're right, I had a choice, but what kind of choice is certain death?"

"What do you mean?" Susan asked.

"The summer I met Sam was the summer I got my draft notice. They wanted to send me to Nam. I'm sure you've heard the stories. I couldn't do it, just couldn't do it." Jessie took the cigarette, grinding the butt angrily into the tree's bark. "Sam was on his way home to Canada, so I went with him. He's been my brother ever since."

"You're a draft dodger? You're older than I thought."

"I get that a lot." Jessie grinned.

"Have you ever gone back home?"

"And face my old man after running away? Not a chance! Add to that the fact that I haven't aged since the 70s. No, I could never explain it to him. So I stayed up here. This is my family now."

"Your family never knew you were a werewolf?" Susan couldn't imagine life without the support of her family.

"Nope. I found out when I met Sam! I don't know what happened really. Maybe it was the stress from my draft notice, maybe it was meeting Sam, or a bunch of different things. Either way, I never looked back."

"That's sad."

Jessie shrugged. "I've made my decisions. I have no one to blame but myself."

Susan curled her knees toward her chest, holding on to the branch for balance. "I know the feeling."

"What do you mean? Please tell me you're not talking about this whole thing with Hunter! There's no way you could have known about him!"

"No, not that. I was thinking about something else." Susan took a deep breath. "Did they tell you how I found out I was a werewolf?"

"We weren't given the details, but we know."

If no one else was going to say it, Susan would, "I killed someone."

"And that's messed up Sue."

"Tell me about it! If I hadn't shifted, or if we hadn't been on the ridge, Jim would still be alive!"

The branch next to Susan creaked. Sam landed beside her. "You can't blame yourself for that Sue."

"You don't get to decide that! You weren't there!"

"No, I wasn't," Sam said in a soothing voice, "But I'm here with you now, and I can tell you would never hurt anyone intentionally."

"How do you know? How could you possibly know what it's like? Have you ever killed someone?"

"Yes." It was the last thing she expected Sam to say. His gaze dropped and his face became old and haggard looking.

"What?" Susan breathed, not sure if she wanted an explanation or not.

Sam's eyes focused on something not quite there in front of them, "I was a soldier in the second world war."

"For real? How old are you? How many wars were you in?"

"That was the only one."

"Do you..." Susan swallowed, a painful lump forming in her throat. "Do you remember killing people?"

"I can still see their faces. Sometimes I dream about it. I've tried to put it behind me, but memories don't listen to your conscience. They pop up when they feel like it. Sometimes it's like living through the whole thing again."

Susan understood. Visions of the night she killed Jim popped into her head at the worst times. All it took was one stupid little thing that reminded her and her brain would go into overdrive. Wind rustled through the branches and they all sat still. Even with the sunlight strong on Susan's face, she felt cold inside.

"Sorry to bring it up." Jessie broke the silence. "You guys have seen things I can only imagine."

"Don't worry about it." Susan let out the breath she had been holding, but her chest remained tight.

"If you ever want to talk about it, come find me, any time." Sam was back to earth, looking Susan in the eye with concern.

"Thank you." Susan didn't know what else to say.

Suddenly, Sam became alert, then Jessie.

An itch crawled up Susan's spine warning her something was wrong. "What is it?"

"Not sure," Sam said. "But it's not good. Evee's pissed about something."

"How do you know?" Susan asked.

"We've been bonded for about a hundred years, I'm pretty good at picking things up."

"Dude," Jessie said, "You don't need to be a genius to pick up that wavelength. Something's got her tail in a knot."

Realization dawned on Susan. "Was that what that tingly feeling in my spine was?"

"Hey, you're catching on lil' sis!" Jessie slapped her shoulder in approval.

"We should go. We're about to be summoned anyway." Sam leapt to the ground.

Jessie followed without hesitation. Susan watched before attempting it herself. The force of hitting the ground was strong, but her body absorbed it effortlessly. She followed the boys inside feeling the knot in her stomach grow.

CHAPTER 17
CHANGES

Evee paced back and forth in front of the door to the meeting room as she waited for the others to arrive. Anna watched her, eyes darting back and forth under dark lashes, from Evee to the floor then back again. Walter had brought her when he intercepted Evee in the hallway. He wouldn't say exactly what was going on with FENRIS, but Evee knew it wasn't good. The way Walter wouldn't look her in the eye told her something was wrong. Then she was told to summon the rest of her pack. Whatever it was would be broken to them as a group, affording her no respect as their leader.

The boys arrived with Susan in tow. Les raised a curious eyebrow, but all Evee could do was shrug in response. She had no answers for them.

The door opened and they were called inside. Evee squared her shoulders, marching into the room to face whatever FENRIS was going to throw at them. Her heart nearly stopped when she saw the pale woman sitting at the head of the table. Evee's hackles rose. She should have known.

"Please have a seat," Came a familiar, snide voice, as the woman lifted her head from her notes. Dark curls fell across her face, refusing to stay in the neat bun pulling back her hair. A ghost of a smile pricked the edges of her red, vampire lips.

Evee wanted to scream, but kept her face expressionless. "Long time no see Lilith. What brings you to my neck of the woods?"

"You mean agent Armstrong, I'm sure." She hung her seniority over Evee's head. "Please have a seat and we'll get right to the heart of the matter."

Evee scraped a chair across the floor, plunking herself directly opposite Lilith. She felt her pack take their seats around her rather than watch them, her eyes trained on the woman opposite her. She knew Lilith – intimately – and her presence here would only spell trouble for her pack.

Les laughed but there was no humour in it, "It had to be you didn't it?"

"You can take up my assignment to this case with the heads of FENRIS if you wish Mr. Burns, but for now, I'm here until the end, one way or another."

Evee's mouth went dry, "You've been assigned to Hunter's case permanently?"

"As the new head of the case I would hope so."

The floor felt like it had been ripped out from underneath Evee. This couldn't be happening.

"Who died and made you boss?" Les didn't bother containing his scorn.

"It's not a death, but lack of results that have promoted me to this position. I don't doubt that the agents who have worked on this case in the past have done so with passion, but if passion could yield results we wouldn't be sitting here now. What this case needs is a tactical mind."

"You mean a soulless bloodsucker!" Les slammed his fist into the table.

"Watch your mouth!" Evee growled at him. If she could contain herself, she expected Les to be on his best behaviour.

The cheshire grin never left Lilith's face. "The bleeding hearts have had their shot. Now it's my turn and I expect full compliance. That won't be a problem for you will it Les?"

"FENRIS will have our full cooperation." Evee answered for him.

"Good," Lilith said, "Because as of this moment you Evelyn and Leslie Burns are stripped of any authority and official involvement in this case. You and your pack are to be treated as civilians..."

The chair clattered to the floor behind Evee as she sprang to her feet, her composure gone. "What?!"

Lilith sighed, "I was afraid you would act like this. Evelyn, this is not your case, it never has been."

"All these years I've given my aid to FENRIS to bring this murderer to justice and that means nothing to you!"

"FENRIS is grateful for your past contributions *and* continued cooperation, but that doesn't mean it's what's best for us right now. I can't let your good intentions get in the way of our success."

"Oh this is rich! Why don't you drive a silver stake through my heart Lil? Finish what you started a hundred years ago!" Evee wanted to crumple to the floor. Only her anger kept her standing.

"Evelyn, this isn't personal. I'm doing what I think is best for everyone."

Evee wanted to scream. She wanted to rip Lilith's smug face off her skull, but that wouldn't change the mess they were in. Worse still, the conniving snake had demoted her right in front of her pack. She couldn't look at her charges, though she could feel their fear and confusion rising through their bond.

"Now, now, it's not all bad news," Lilith's tone was anything but reassuring. "In fact you may be pleased to know that Susan's adjudicator has arrived and we can begin the process of assessing her."

"We can't start now!" Les rose at Evee's side, "Not with all the stress Susan is under! I move we postpone Susan's assessment until Hunter is caught and the danger has passed."

"Overruled." Lilith sat cold and still as a statue, unmoved by Les' outburst. "I am aware of the extreme circumstances regarding this assessment, but given how long the process is, I see no reason to delay. You wouldn't want to keep Adolphus waiting would you?"

A spark of hope lit in Evee's chest. Perhaps not everything was bad news after all. She straightened herself, reaffirming her command. "No. We won't keep him waiting."

"Excellent. I'll let him make arrangements with you as he likes." Lilith jotted some notes on a piece of paper in front of her, ignoring the pack.

"Are we done?" Evee wanted to get out of the room.

"Don't you want to know what the plan is regarding Hunter?" Lilith asked without looking up from her notes.

"I didn't think us civilians would be privy to such matters." Evee sneered.

"I think it's to our benefit to keep you informed. Well, to a certain extent anyway." Lilith rose from her seat and made her way around the table to where Anna sat, leaning toward the girl, inspecting her. "So this is the target?"

Evee had to unclench her jaw to speak. "Anna Russel."

"You're lucky to have joined us Anna. I understand things have been uncertain for you, but you're safe now under my jurisdiction."

Anna said nothing, avoiding Lilith's gaze. Reaching forward, Lilith curled a finger under Anna's chin lifting her face until their eyes met. "She's cute too, but then you always had good taste Evelyn."

Evee felt her claws digging into her palms, the urge to knock Lilith's head off her body rising. "She's also a minor under my care, so I'd appreciate you keeping your grubby paws off her!"

Lilith drew back laughing, "Oh Evelyn, I'd like to say, 'Well I never' but..." She ran her eyes over Evee, "Well, case in point..."

"Weren't you going to tell us something useful?" Les stepped between them. "Like what your plans are?"

Lilith pursed her lips, weighing her words, "Well right now we have the advantage don't we? Given our position, the next move is Hunter's and we're going to wait and see what he does."

"That's it?" Evee was tired of being toyed with. "That's your grand plan? We're supposed to sit around and wait?"

"That's what you're going to be doing yes. Don't worry, FENRIS will not be idle, but the less you know of the details behind the scenes the better."

"So that's it? You drag us in here to tell us there's nothing we can do but sit and wait while Hunter makes a play for our lives?"

Lilith wandered slowly back to her seat on the other side of the table. "Patience never was your strong suit Evee. Yes, for now you are going to wait, obediently, until our situation changes. Is that clear to all of you?"

"Crystal." Evee spoke for her pack.

"You should consider yourselves lucky I've allowed you so many freedoms. Of course, anyone who can't follow FENRIS directions will be put into solitary confinement. But that won't be an issue, will it?" Lilith looked at each pack member in turn, daring them to defy her.

Silence permeated the room. Evee folded her arms across her chest.

"Good." Lilith took her seat again, going back to her notes. "Guards will be posted to watch the girls twenty-four-seven. If you need anything, please feel free to let me know. You are dismissed."

Evee stormed out the room, fuming, but didn't open her mouth until she was well out of earshot. "That impossible bloodsucker!" She raised her fists into the air, resisting the urge to slam them through the walls.

"What was that all about?" Susan whispered to Les.

"Evee and Lilith have a history."

"Thank you Captain Obvious! What about?"

"It was a long time ago." Evee faced Susan. As much as she didn't want to relive old memories, the girls deserved an explanation. "After Hunter took my first love away from me, I found solace with Lilith for a while."

"What?!" Susan shrieked. "You guys were involved like *that*?!"

"That explains a lot," Anna shivered. "I didn't like the way she looked at me."

Evee saw red. "That's because that woman is a snake! She'd eat you alive if she could and spit you back out for the sake of watching you squirm."

"Nothing like a burned lover's scorn..." Les tried to make light of things.

"I wouldn't add fuel to the fire," Sam warned him.

The wave of anger passed and Evee composed herself. "Well, we can't change the situation right now, but don't think I'm not going to try! My first responsibility is to all of you, and I'm going to protect you no matter what."

The faces around Evee ranged from hopeful to unsure. She couldn't blame them. Doubt nagged at her own confidence, but she'd be damned if she gave up that easily. When she looked at Les, a knowing glance passed between them.

"You should go," he said. "Do what you need to do." It was her brother's way of telling her she should go blow off some steam before she tore down the walls around them.

Evee nodded her thanks and left them in the hall, her feet taking her through the school without thinking, until she reached a remote corner of the building. She fumbled through a set of keys, her hands trembling as she put one in the lock and gave it a turn. The door opened revealing an empty room before her. The windows on the far side stretched almost to the ceiling, letting cascades of afternoon sunlight wash the floor.

Evee shut the door behind her, walking slowly towards a boombox across the room. Her reflection walked with her, cut in half by a barre at her midsection. Evee fumbled through a series of tapes before realizing the one she wanted was already in the machine. The play button sank under her finger and she cranked the volume.

Relief washed over her as Evee walked to the middle of the empty dance floor, shaking off the last bit of wolf becoming fully human again. She became aware of her body, the flexing of each muscle, the tension that had built in her shoulders. She needed to let that go. Toes pointed, arms poised, she danced through the room, losing herself in the motion. Here she could be as aggressive or incorrect as she wanted. She took her hurt and anger, channeling it through her body to make something beautiful as she danced away.

During a spin, Evee caught sight of the open door and someone watching her. She stiffened and Anna's scent hit her nose. The girl stood wide eyed, frozen with one hand still pushing the door open.

"Well, don't stand in the doorway!" Evee snapped. "Come in and close it behind you."

"Sorry! I didn't mean to interrupt!" Anna stumbled in, shutting the door.

"I'm done anyway." Evee ran her fingers through sweat soaked hair. "What are you doing up here anyway?"

"Les sent me. We wanted to know if you were coming down to dinner?"

"Is it that late already?" Evee saw the setting sun through the windows. Time had flown while she worked out her anger.

"I didn't know you liked to dance." Anna inspected the room, but her eyes kept darting apprehensively in Evee's direction.

Evee watched the girl's guarded glances, reading a familiar body language. Anna was shy but there was an interest and curiosity there aimed at Evee. It was something Evee knew she should quash, but she couldn't find it in her to put Anna through anything more than she had been through already.

"There's a lot you don't know about me," Evee said.

"As I keep finding out." Anna paused, waiting expectantly for Evee to say more.

"I'm sorry about Lilith." Evee blurted out. "I had no idea she was going to be there."

"It's not your fault," Anna said, running a hand over the barre.

"No, but it is my job to protect you, and if I could help it, I'd keep that woman as far away from you as possible!"

"She seems to enjoy getting under people's skin."

"She's always been like that! But usually she's far more reserved and charming when it comes to first impressions. Then again, maybe she was forward with you for the sake of getting under my skin."

"I can't believe you dated someone like that!"

"People aren't always what they seem at first."

"That's true. I was thinking though," Anna finally met Evee's eyes, "It's probably a good thing we have her working on the case."

"You see a bright side to all of this that I missed?"

Anna chewed her bottom lip, eyes returning to the floor. "She reminds me of Hunter. There's something about her, the way she acts, the way she's full of herself. Maybe what we need is someone who thinks like him, and maybe that's why Lilith was picked for this case."

"From the mouths of babes!" Evee couldn't believe it. Anna had done more to reassure her in minutes than dancing had done for her in hours. "I suppose FENRIS is trying to fight fire with fire. Not that I'm sure it'll work..."

"Are you sure it won't?"

"We'll see how it plays out won't we?"

CHAPTER 18
LEGENDS

Susan tugged at the collar of her shirt which felt too tight around her thick werewolf neck. Evee stood in front of her, straightening her own shirt collar before rapping on the guest room door. The formality of it all itched at Susan's skin. She and Evee were expected to be in their werewolf forms, dressed neatly and on their best behaviour. They were about to have a preliminary meeting with Susan's adjudicator. It was bad enough to be in the situation they were in with Hunter, but the fact that FENRIS wouldn't delay her assessment made Susan even more nervous. Anna stood a pace behind them. She had been summoned as well, though Susan wasn't sure if it was to keep a close eye on her, or for some other reason.

Everyone snapped to attention when a small grey werewolf opened the door. She sniffed at each of them in turn before opening it wide enough to admit them. "We've been expecting you. Please come in."

Susan's throat was too dry to swallow and the air around her too thin. Her head swam as Evee marched into the room and Susan followed close behind, using Evee to shield her from whatever lay inside. She could feel Anna behind her, but her best friend's presence offered little comfort in this situation.

Susan stood for a moment, taking in the cozy sitting room they had entered. The morning light peeked through cracks in the curtains warming an ornate set of furniture surrounding a coffee table laden with treats. Plates of cookies and slices of cake filled the room with a comforting scent, and a silver pot sat steaming with fresh tea. This was the last thing Susan expected. She never would have guessed her interrogator's tools of torture would be tea and crumpets.

Anna took a seat on the couch and Susan sat beside her. The cushion beneath her barely gave way and Susan realized the furniture was built more for looks than comfort. The chairs didn't seem any better as Evee grumbled trying to settle into one. It was just as well. There was no way Susan was going to be at ease for this meeting.

The werewolf who greeted them rushed off into an adjoining room. She returned with an elderly wolf-man leaning on her arm. The hairs on the back of Susan's neck rose. Despite his obvious age, he had a powerful scent about him, like an ancient forest, old and resinous.

The old werewolf moved slowly, testing his footing as he let himself be led to the empty chair next to Susan. His cloudy white eyes did not focus, but he still turned his head to face each of his guests, his nose quivering.

The young wolf at his side poured a cup of tea, setting it in front of him. "Will you need anything else Grandfather?"

"No darling," He shooed her away. "I can take care of myself and I'd like to speak to our guests in private."

"Of course." She left the room, leaving silence in her wake.

After a moment the old wolf motioned at the coffee table, "Please help yourselves."

Susan grabbed a plate and a piece of cake, but her hand hovered above the table as she realized there was no type of refreshment suitable for Anna. Evee got up to pour tea for herself and Susan, giving Anna an apologetic look and a warning glare at Susan not to make a fuss.

"It's good to see you again Evelyn!" The old werewolf winced trying to settle in his chair. "I see Red Oaks still has poor taste in furniture."

"Only for our most prestigious guests!" Evee sat, placing her cup and saucer in her lap. "Of course it's not like I have a say in the decor."

"No? I thought you were still on the board here?"

"Replacing the guest room furniture hasn't exactly been a priority."

"Hmph, I suppose some things never change." He turned to Susan but didn't look at her directly, "You must be the young Miss Wolfe?"

"Yes sir!" Susan didn't mean to jump, but it was hard to keep calm. The old wolf's eyes didn't focus on her, but Susan could swear they were staring at her. Coupled with his scent, Susan found herself completely intimidated by the blind old man.

"Now, now," He waved his hand in her general direction, "No need to be frightened by a dotty old man like myself! You've been told no doubt that I am here to judge your deeds and assess your threat to our community, but please allow me to introduce myself. I'm Adolphus."

"Susan Wolfe."

The old wolf turned his nose toward Anna. "And this must be the new vampire child? Miss Russel was it?"

"Yes. Thank you for inviting me." Anna sat gripping the edge of the cushion, looking skeptically at Susan.

"No trouble at all my dear! I was curious to meet the vampire who managed to become a member of the illustrious Burns pack!"

"Was that sarcasm old man?" Evee laughed.

"Now Evelyn, you do yourself a disservice."

"I know there's a ruckus going on about it, but given the pack history, can you honestly say you're surprised?"

The old wolf laughed. "True. True."

"What do you mean?" Anna asked.

"Your children really have no idea about our world do they?" Adolphus placed his cup and saucer on the table and sat back tenting his fingers together.

"Do you think we've had time to teach them with everything that's going on?" Evee said.

"Well it's a good thing you brought them both then. You two are in sore need of a few lessons in the ways and history of our peoples."

"Like what?" Susan mumbled through a bite of cake, curiosity trumping her anxiety.

Adolphus raised an eyebrow, folding his hands together in his lap. "Traditionally vampires and werewolves don't mix, at least not on the family level. We stick to our packs and they to their houses. Only recently have the two been adopting each other and even then, it's usually younger children forming new families. The oldest packs and houses have been somewhat reticent to change."

"Have you ever known me to play by the rules old man?" Evee sipped her tea.

"Of course not! Everyone thought it strange when you wanted to adopt Les, but then you kept adopting strays. Stranger still they were not even your own kind! The old packmasters thought you had lost your mind!"

"Wait," Something didn't sit right with Susan, "So, having a pack of different animals is weird? We're not normal?"

"I've always thought of us as progressive," Evee said. "You would think werewolves would be more open to change and accepting other's differences, but old traditions die hard. Usually packs stay within families, which means wolves stick with wolves. Only recently have some of us expanded our horizons."

"Great," Anna said under her breath, "Even among werewolves we're freaks!"

Adolphus leaned toward Anna, "Do you think being different is a bad thing?"

Anna hesitated before answering, "It usually leads to trouble."

"Yes, it can lead to trouble," The old wolf leaned back into his chair again, "Or it can lead to opportunity. Some people think of werewolves as being cursed. Indeed, we are subject to a beast we cannot always control, and are capable of terrible things. But many of us choose to see being a werewolf as a Gift. We are all capable of great or terrible things, it's what we do with the Gift that matters."

"So where did this Gift come from then?" Susan asked the first thing that came to mind, keeping the conversation away from her.

"Where do you think we come from Susan?" Adolphus asked her.

"I don't know. I haven't really thought about it. Werewolf stories are so old and you talk about us like we've been around forever.

"Yes the stories about us are old! It's hard to imagine a time without stories of shape-shifters. Some say we evolved alongside humans for thousands of years, but there's a more popular story and it's one I'm partial to." Adolphus paused, reaching for his tea cup.

"What is it?" Susan took the bait. Anything to keep the old wolf going.

"Ah, the impatience of youth!" Adolphus took a sip of his tea, but there was a twinkle in his eye as if he found something amusing in Susan's curiosity. "The truth is, we don't know much about our origins at all. Stories have been passed down in every family since the dawn of mankind, but one thing is consistent in all of them, humans were here first, and we came from them. I like this idea because it means we are all fundamentally human, no matter how strong our inner beast."

Adolphus took another sip of tea and Susan restrained herself from prodding him further. He set his cup on the table and his gaze became distant.

"The story tells us, when man was young and close to the earth, he was friends with the beasts. Different tribes had bonds with different animals, and because of these deep friendships the animals bestowed their Gifts upon man. Each animal selected a handful of humans and granted them their abilities. These humans gained strength, wisdom and longevity and could change themselves into their patron animal if they wished. These humans were meant to watch over their tribes, to guide them to live in harmony with their animal kin.

"However, through the ages, man changed. He forgot himself and the sacred connection with his brothers and sisters. Tribes scattered and mixed. Humans forgot their duty and their friendships. We grew apart from the animals, becoming lost in the new societies humans created."

"Does that mean we weren't always a secret?" Susan asked.

"In this story, no we started out as a respected part of the tribe. In fact some ancient cultures seemed to venerate the link between animals and humans, but whether this is true or not, who can say? Over time celebration of our power and wisdom waned and gave way to fear. For how many centuries has the wolf been a villain in human tales, a manifestation of fear, hunger and evil?"

"But how could we go from one extreme to the other?" Susan asked.

"Fear is a powerful force, never to be underestimated. You should know that first hand."

Susan's throat tightened and her questions died on her lips. Memories flashed before her eyes of fear taking over her body and transforming her into a monster. Fear could change someone in a heartbeat. It could do terrible things to people.

Adolphus' voice gently brought Susan back to the room, "Of course the other side of our emotional nature is that we have a great depth for compassion."

"If only that was easier to tap into!" Susan realized she was being a bit more candid than she should be, but if the old wolf minded he gave no indication.

"We become what we practice," he said. "The more you exercise your compassion and challenge your fears the better you become at controlling them."

"But what if I make a mistake? What if I hurt someone in the process?" Susan searched Adolphus' grey face for any hint of absolution, but it remained an unreadable mask.

His voice however, was kind when he spoke. "We all make mistakes child, what matters is what you do after you make one."

Susan decided it was time to drop any pretence she might have still had. It was time to lay everything on the table. "I don't know that that matters. I can't fix what I've done. I can't bring Jim back."

"True, you can't change the past." The old wolf paused, weighing his words, "But you do have control over yourself in the present. Do you let doubt cripple your mind? Do you let your fear own you, or do you allow yourself to accept compassion?"

These weren't the kind of questions Susan expected from her adjudicator. He wasn't so much judging her as guiding her. "Is this some sort of test? I don't ever want to lose myself like that again. It was horrible. But I can't forgive myself either. I keep thinking about Jim and his family and what I've done. To be honest, I don't know what to do with myself."

"Hmm," Adolphus' nose quivered in Susan's direction, "I've lived for so many years, sometimes I forget how long it takes wounds like these to heal. It can heal if you let it, or it can fester and take over your life. While you have been through something horrible Susan, you must not let it consume you."

"Easier said than done."

"No one is suggesting it will be easy."

Anna's hand touched Susan's arm. Nothing about their lives was easy at that moment, but at least they had each other.

"So, where do vampires fit into all this?" Susan changed the subject.

The fur around Adolphus' eyes crinkled. Susan couldn't tell if he was smiling or scrutinizing her. "Vampires were not among the original tribes. They are... products of a certain group of wolf children."

"You mean we were made?" Anna's interest piqued.

"Not quite. Unmade might be a better way to put it, but let me tell the tale. There once was a group of brothers, fierce warriors, renowned throughout the lands for their strength in battle. They were proud of their ties with the wolf, but their power and fame corrupted them. They began to revel in bloodshed, slaughtering their enemies without mercy. After one battle the warriors destroyed everything. They left nothing alive in their wake and burned everything that remained to the ground. This destruction and disregard for life, angered the spirit of the wolf that the brothers claimed to emulate. So the Wolf spirit cursed these men, that they should know a thirst only blood could slake, and that only by the moon's light could they hunt. The light of the sun would burn their flesh and force them into the darkness that had consumed them." Adolphus paused tilting his face away from Anna. "Lastly, vampires cannot bear children of their own, though they can inflict others with their curse."

"That's a sad story." Anna dropped her gaze to her lap.

"But vampires are still strong and fast and live long lives like us right?" Susan tried to pick out something positive to hang on to. "So did they really have their Gift taken away?"

"It's hard to say for certain," Adolphus mused. "Some say the Gift could not be rescinded, only changed."

"What about their ability to shift?" Susan asked.

"Aha! A point of much contention!" Adolphus jabbed a claw in the air. "As far as we know, vampires could still adopt the wolf's form, or at least they used to be able to."

"Don't fill their heads with nonsense!" Evee bared her teeth in distaste, but was careful not to look at Adolphus while doing so.

"Now Evelyn, just because you haven't seen it doesn't mean it's not true!"

"No one has seen a vampire shift for hundreds of years!"

"I have seen it," Adolphus said. "Once in my youth. A strange and incredible thing. Sadly, the art has been lost among modern vampires."

"How do you forget how to shift?" Susan couldn't understand. Shifting was supposed to get easier with practice, not harder, and for the ability to disappear completely was an unsettling thought.

"Well, the mechanism for shifting seems to be different for vampires than for werewolves. The key to their transformation continues to elude us, though certainly not from lack of trying."

"It's a popular topic among the younger generations," Evee snorted. "However the elders feel like trying to figure it out is a waste of time."

"Or they are discouraged and have given up on themselves," Adolphus said. "I've always thought of it as a redeeming clause in the vampire curse. As you are aware, some vampires are made through entirely no fault of their own, and many question why they should pay for the sins of the past. It is said that the wolf form is a reward for the most virtuous of vampires because it enables them to walk under the sun without burning!"

"Saying that is like saying every vampire in existence today deserves the curse of their forefathers because they can't shift!" Evee struggled to keep the growl from her voice. "How can you put that kind of pressure on them?"

"Now, now, no one really knows the truth of the matter."

"Then don't fill their heads with rumours and fairy tales!" Evee snapped.

"And why not?" Adolphus grinned, baring his teeth in Evee's direction. "Perhaps what we need most is a fresh perspective. Just because the method is lost does not mean it can't be relearned, or better yet, reinvented! I'm telling the children fairy tales not to make them feel inadequate but to inspire them. I don't know about you, but I'm excited to see what they come up with!"

CHAPTER 19
LETTER

Susan's feet pounding across the floor echoed through the halls as she ran toward where she felt Evee would be. The tingle in her spine told her something was wrong. Arguing voices spilled out of an open door and Susan found herself outside what must have been Evee's study.

A FENRIS agent stood alert at the doorway, raising a hand at Susan as she approached. He went to bar her way, but Susan stopped at the threshold. Another agent was inside, bagging and labelling a piece of paper, while Lilith and Evee stood staring each other down.

"I don't care how obvious a ploy it is! We have to do something!" Evee's white fur stood on end making her look larger than usual.

"We are," Lilith responded as calm and cool as ever, "But that doesn't mean head on confrontation."

"It was addressed to me, not you, not FENRIS!" Evee growled.

"Of course he sent it to *you!*" Lilith reached for the now protected piece of paper. "You're the most likely to defy orders and play right into his hands!"

Evee threw her hands in the air. "And did I do that? No! I called you first, like I'm supposed to. I'm cooperating!"

"Congratulations. Would you like a medal or something?" Lilith's sarcasm was scathing. "Your cooperation is expected."

"Then take my advice Lil," Evee took a step toward her, "Use this as an opportunity to catch him!"

Lilith ignored her, staring at the piece of paper, "That's exactly what he wants us to do Evee. We're not going to rush into anything without thinking through the possibilities."

"We'll miss our window!"

"Again, that's what he wants you to think. Use your head for once, not your heart!" Lilith finally looked toward the door, acknowledging Susan's presence, "Calling the herd are we?"

"It's not like I'm trying to hide my frustration." Evee crossed her arms over her chest.

Susan's mouth went dry. "What's going on?"

Evee walked over to her. "I got an invitation to a private party, just Hunter and me."

"Which you are not going to follow up on." Lilith made her orders clear. "FENRIS will take it from here."

"And how long will that take Lil?"

"It takes as long as it takes to get the job done right. I think we have everything we need. You're dismissed."

"Then get out of my office!" Evee yelled.

Lilith strolled out of the study, followed by the two agents who quickly gathered their things.

"What was that all about?" Susan let out a breath she had been holding. She searched the tiny room and the white werewolf for clues, but none were forthcoming.

Evee sighed, placing a hand on Susan's shoulder. "It's her way of saying 'don't get in my way.' And she's right. We shouldn't disrupt the case."

"Don't we get a say in what happens?"

"If we're lucky." Evee wouldn't meet her charge's eyes. "Come on. We need to have a meeting."

"Were you calling us before, or was that a gut feeling I had?" Susan reflected on Lilith's words.

"Part of the bond means being connected to the emotions of your pack mates," Evee explained. "When one of us is afraid or in pain, it usually reaches out to the others, sort of like a warning."

"That's cool... but kind of weird. What if you don't want the others to know what you're feeling?"

"Well," Evee said, "You can learn to block things out so the others don't notice."

"Is that hard to learn?"

Evee grinned, "It takes practice, along with everything else. But right now, I'd appreciate knowing if you were in any kind of trouble."

Susan couldn't argue with that. There were a lot of quirks she had to get used to, but at least she could see where this one would come in handy. She let Evee lead her to a small meeting room where the pack gathered. They sat together in the dull light of the drawn curtains until Les broke the silence.

"What's up? Does FENRIS have a new lead or something?"

"Yes, there's been a new development." Evee folded her hands in front of her on the table, maintaining a calm expression.

"And we aren't being briefed? Wonderful!" Les drummed his fingers on the table.

Evee sat up straight, commanding everyone's attention, "Lilith assumes – and rightly so – that I'll tell you about this. She's not going to officially pass on this knowledge. It would be too dangerous."

"Dangerous?" Sam tilted his head. "How?"

"Let me start from the beginning," Evee said. "I received a letter this morning from Hunter, 'inviting' me to a one on one challenge to end things once and for all between us."

Les snorted, "Could he be any more obvious in setting a trap for you?"

"Hardly. He's counting on my ego to overpower my

common sense. However, this would seem like the perfect opportunity to set a trap of our own and turn the tables. Lilith won't tell me anything though. I have no idea what FENRIS intends on doing with this information, if anything."

"So what do you have planned?" Les asked.

Evee remained rigid, "I'm still trying to appeal to the higher-ups to get some control back, but it's taking too long. Right now we have a good idea where Hunter is and that he's waiting for me. I'd hate to waste this opportunity."

"Don't you dare!" A shock ran through the room as Anna admonished Evee.

Evee gaped at the girl, her jaw hanging slightly open.

"Evee," Anna said, "If anything happens to you, or anyone else for that matter, because you're trying to protect me, I'll never forgive myself. Please don't do anything!"

Evee suddenly looked old, the wear of long years hanging on her features, "This isn't just about you Anna. Hunter's hurt me far more than you can imagine."

"Which is even more reason to step back and let FENRIS do their job." Anna refused to back down.

Evee's eyes were distant and glassy when she spoke, "I would gladly sacrifice myself to see an end to this."

"Don't say that!" Anna rose to her feet, shaking in distress. "No one has to get hurt! We have to be patient!"

"And how long will you wait?" Evee glared at Anna. "Years? Decades? What's to say Hunter doesn't disappear off the face of the earth for a hundred years, only to torment you and everyone else until we all go mad! I won't be held captive for the rest of my life when I know I could put and end to this!"

"Evee, listen to yourself," Les said, "We all need to calm down and think about this. I'm sure we can come up with a reasonable plan together."

Evee slumped forward, resting her face in her hands, her eyes closed. An uncomfortable silence filled the room.

Eventually Evee's eyes opened and she sat back. "You're both right. I need to think about this and what we should do. I need some time to myself, if the rest of you don't mind."

Chairs scraped the floor as everyone rose to make a hasty exit from the meeting room. Susan glanced over her shoulder as she left, but Evee hadn't moved, sitting as still and frightening as a gargoyle, her cold eyes boring a hole into space.

Ψ

Susan bolted upright in her bed. Pain stabbed her chest and a sick feeling rushed to her head. It took her a moment to realize that though the pain was real it was not hers. The relief that had begun to wash over her went cold. Beside her, in their darkened dorm room, Anna also sat up clutching her chest. Their eyes met.

"Evee!" Anna gasped.

Susan swore and ripped the covers off. She vaulted out of bed, and ran to the door, tearing it open, but then stopped, realizing she had no idea where she was going.

"The entrance hall." Anna came up beside her. "It's the closest place between everyone."

"At least one of us is getting good at this 'bond' thing." Susan wasted no time running down the hall toward the stairs. She could hear the stirring of FENRIS agents in the room across from theirs. It didn't matter. They could do what they liked, but Susan needed to see the faces of her pack mates. She needed to smell them, feel them, know that they were real and safe because there was growing doubt in her heart they were.

The girls were the last to arrive. Cold seeped through the windows and doors, creating a draft that made Susan shiver. The faces of the three boys in the hall did nothing to comfort her. They were all drawn with worry. Les was pale, but smiled when he saw them. Everyone moved close together reaching out to touch the others.

"What's going on?" Anna trembled as she wrapped her arms around Les.

"Yes, what's happened and where's Evelyn?" From the open gallery a floor above, Lilith was watching them.

"What, you mean she managed to get around your security detail?" Les sounded genuinely surprised.

Lilith jumped the full storey over the gallery railing, landing neatly beside the pack. "Save your scorn Leslie. Out with it. Where is she?" Other agents began to surround the hall.

"I don't know," Les said.

"And yet it's clear that something happened or you all wouldn't be standing here."

"I don't know where she is," Tears threatened in Les' eyes. "I don't know what she's done, but I do know there was nothing that would have stopped her from taking this whole mess on her shoulders. You know her. You of all people. Did you really think she'd sit quietly by with the chance to end things being waved in her face?"

Lilith swore under her breath. "Is she dead?"

"No," Les swallowed thickly, "But she's wounded and terrified. That much I can feel."

"Great! We had him right where we wanted him..."

"Then why didn't you tell us!" Les screamed in her face. "This is your fault Lilith! If you had told Evee what you were doing she wouldn't have tried to finish this on her own!"

Lilith approached Les, shoving her face within inches of his, her voice low and threatening, "Not another word."

"Fine!" Les threw his hands up in surrender, "Then why don't you tell us, oh powerful one, what the plan is to rescue my sister and fix this mess?"

Lilith drew back, eyeing each pack member in turn. "There is no plan."

"Why not?!" Les demanded.

"Don't you get it? She played right into his trap! He's going to use her to bait the rest of you and get exactly what he wants." Lilith's gaze settled on Anna. "Evee's on her own."

"What?!" Susan couldn't believe what she was hearing. "You can't do this! You can't leave her out there! She's going to die!" No one had said it, but she knew they could all feel it. Though the sharpness of the pain subsided, she could feel Evee's connection growing weaker. "We could find her! We could save her!"

"You will do no such thing," Lilith said. "Especially you and Anna."

"Let me go then," Les stepped forward. "You can give me a team or not, it doesn't matter."

"No, I'm not giving him any more power than he's already gained. If you don't agree to cooperate and let me handle this, I'll have you restrained."

"You'll need to lock me in a silver cage to keep me from going after her." Les shifted and openly bared his teeth at her.

"If that's what it takes." Lilith waved a hand and two agents stepped away from the edge of the room, grabbing Les by the arms. Susan gasped as someone pulled at her own arm. Each of them were surrounded and then the agents began to pull them away from each other.

CHAPTER 20
THE HUNT

"We have to do something! We can't just sit here!" Susan slammed her fist into the closed door of their dorm room, hoping the sound would startle any FENRIS agents who might be listening. Someone would now be posted on the other side of the door at all times. Her skin crawled in frustration.

"There's nothing we can do. Calm down." Anna said, surprisingly placid.

"Calm down! Sure, when my chest stops throbbing and everyone is safe! Then I'll calm down!"

Anna moved over to her desk, soundlessly scribbling a note on a piece of paper. *I feel the same. I want to go out there, but we have to be smart about it.*

Susan's ears twitched at the shuffling outside the door. She nodded.

"I know it's hard, but what do you want to do?" Anna continued the charade, "Run out there and get caught, or worse? You know he'll kill us if he finds us!" She handed the pen and paper to Susan.

Got any ideas? Susan wrote.

Anna grinned and pointed at the ceiling. Susan stared perplexed, then kicked herself. Anna wasn't pointing at the ceiling, she meant the roof. They were on the third floor. It couldn't be hard to get out the window and onto the roof. From there they could cross the building and find an opening in the wall of FENRIS agents surrounding them.

"I need some air. This is killing me." Susan crossed the room and ripped the window pane up. The opening was small but she was sure they could fit through it. Shapes on the ground caught Susan's eye and she pounded a fist on the sill. Grabbing the pen she jotted: *They're outside. They'll see us.*

How many? Anna wrote back.

Susan sniffed the air wafting through the opening. *Two close by but there might be more.* She hesitated before adding, *Are you sure about this? This is exactly what he wants us to do.*

Evee saved my life. I'd be dead right now if it wasn't for her. She wouldn't give up if one of us was out there.

She also wouldn't want you to throw your life away!

I didn't have a choice when Will changed me but I have a choice right now. If there's even a small chance of saving her life it's worth it.

"Damn you got it bad!" Susan teased.

"Shut up! Are you going to 'calm down' or not?"

"Seeing as how we're stuck together in this room until FENRIS gets their butts in gear, I guess I don't have a choice. I don't like it, but..." Susan searched for words that wouldn't be too revealing, "I'll follow your lead."

"Thank you!" Anna wrapped her arms around Susan's shoulders burying her face in her hair. Susan let Anna hold her for a while, as they stood in silence. Slowly Susan pulled away, holding a finger to her lips and hit the light switch. "Let's go to bed. Things will be better in the morning."

"I hope you're right."

Susan removed her clothes and shifted into a werewolf,

crouching on the edge of her bed. They waited in silence. Minutes trickled by, feeling like hours. The darkness outside the window increased. The sky became clouded and moonless, perfect for getting lost to sight.

They waited until the draft from the window brought new smells to Susan's nose. The agents were changing their shift. She held up her hand and Anna crept forward, careful not to reveal herself to anyone below. Susan kept herself hidden in the shadows as she crept to the window and peeked over the sill. The world outside was silent and black. She couldn't see the agents, but her instincts told her this would probably be the best opportunity they would get. Anna's dark eyes stood out from her skin, pale even in the shadows. Determination stared back at her. Susan nodded once and tensed taking a deep breath. It was now or never.

Susan crawled out the window, pulling herself up onto the ledge. She jumped and caught the eaves, swinging herself up to the roof in a single motion. Anna was right behind her, springing from the ledge and catching Susan's hand as she pulled her up to the roof. A horrible grating sound rent the darkness as Anna scrambled on the shingles. It wasn't all that loud, but the girls cringed as it shattered the silence.

They took off running immediately, their footfalls pattering down the roof like rain. The further they ran from their room the bolder they became, leaping from roof tops and scrambling across shingles. Susan had reached the end of a roof low enough to jump to the ground, when a howl pierced the air. Their escape had been discovered.

Susan bolted down the roof, leaping from the edge to the frozen ground below. She tumbled as she hit the ground, rolling forward, finding her feet and pushing off in a sprint for the tree line. Shouts and howls were now echoing in the field behind her, but the shelter of the trees muffled the mayhem. Once in the trees, Susan stopped, checking behind her. Anna was right at her heels, jumping past her, melding into the shadows of the forest.

"And you didn't want to try out for the cross-country team?!" Susan scoffed.

Anna called back, "I think vampire superpowers might be improving my time! Come on, we can't stop now!"

Susan threw herself down to all fours, and caught up with Anna in no time. Every second was critical. The howling became more distant, but then it ceased abruptly. Susan halted in her tracks, turning back the way they had come.

Anna reeled in the snow, coming back to where Susan stood sniffing the air. "What's wrong?"

"They stopped."

"Why?"

"They probably don't want to alert Hunter, or us."

"Do you think we lost them?"

The hair on the back of Susan's neck prickled. "No. Either they're trailing us quietly or..."

"Or Lilith called them off. I don't think she'll let us go that easily."

"No, but it's going to force her to change her plans. We might be nothing more than a calculated loss to her."

Anna shuddered, "Screw her! How are we going to find Evee? She could be anywhere."

"You know that's not true. Can't you feel her pulling at your heart." A deep ache throbbed in Susan's chest in sympathy with whatever pain Evee was going through at Hunter's hand.

"Yes! We have to open up to the bond and..." Anna clutched her chest. Her knees wobbled and gave way as she sank into the snow. Her breathing came out ragged, but she screwed her eyes shut, clenched her fists and regained her composure. "I... I can't... she's in pain! I can't focus on her! I can't find her!"

"It's OK," Susan didn't want Anna to panic. "We don't

need an exact location right now, just a general direction. I'd try but..."

"I know it's scary." Anna pulled herself to her feet.

"That's not what I was going to say. You're better at this feeling stuff, and... I think your bond with Evee is stronger."

Anna ran her hand over her face, instinctively trying to hide her blush. "I think it's easier for me because of the turning."

"Then use that! Remember what you told me about how people have an essence? Maybe focus more on that and not on what Evee's going through right now."

"I'll try." Anna closed her eyes placing her hands protectively over her heart. Her face twitched, but she stood firm. Then her eyes flashed open staring through the trees at a spot in the distance. "That way."

They took off, galloping between the trees. The painful tugging at Susan's heart became harder to ignore the closer they approached. She couldn't get a grasp on the distance though. The intensity of Evee's pain was muddling her senses.

Anna paused. She remained focused on a spot in the distance, but her voice dropped to a whisper, "We're close."

"This is it then. You know we're walking straight into his territory?"

"I don't care if it's a trap, I can't leave Evee out here. I'm not going to let her suffer and I'm sure as Hell not going to let her die because of me."

Susan butted her head into Anna's side and Anna wrapped her arms around Susan's neck.

"I won't let him win this time." Anna ran her fingers through Susan's fur. "Promise me something Sue. Promise me you'll get him. No matter what happens to me, or Evee or anyone else."

Susan felt the pit of her stomach drop away. "You want me to let the beast out? What if I hurt you? What if I can't control it?"

"I trust you."

"I'm glad one of us does."

"I mean it! I trust you. I know, you won't hurt me or Evee and I know you're strong enough to do this! Promise me, you won't let him get away."

Letting her feral instinct take over was the one thing Susan never wanted to experience again, but it might be the only way to end this. "I promise I'll do whatever I have to to save you and Evee."

"OK." Anna pulled back, wiping tears from her eyes. "I have an idea. Let me go in first. I'll distract him."

"But you're the one he wants!"

"Exactly! He'll be too focused on me to care about anything else! While he's distracted you come up from behind. He can't take on both of us at once."

"I don't like this."

"Do you have any better ideas?"

Susan took a deep breath, the cold air burning her lungs. "No."

"This is it then. The boys are probably under lock and key and no one else is going to save us. It's all up to us." Anna began walking away, but stopped after a few steps. "Sue, thank you."

It sounded too much like a goodbye for Susan's liking, but before she could protest, Anna was gone, running towards the spot where Evee lay, and probably Hunter too. Susan waited a few agonizing moments, letting Anna get a head start. Then she began to stalk silently through the trees. Her senses were pricked, her bonds open, ready to receive whatever cues she could from Anna or Evee.

A shiver of fear ran through Susan's heart and she knew Anna had found Hunter. She quickened her pace, then his scent came trailing in on the wind. Voices echoed through the dark woods, but Susan couldn't make out words. She approached from downwind, coming to the edge of a hollow where a fallen tree had torn a hole in the canopy of branches, revealing the sky above. The clouds had moved on, leaving a trail of stars in their wake, dimly lighting the clearing.

There he was, sitting on top of the trunk of that massive fallen tree, Hunter. Anna stood out of reach at the edge of the clearing. It seemed far, but Anna knew better than to get too close. Susan could smell Anna's fear and Hunter's excitement, but then another scent slammed into her nostrils. Blood. And it was fresh. The sound of her own blood pumping through her veins began to beat in her ears and the world turned from shades of black to red.

Susan shoved her nose into the snow. It was cold and clean smelling, purging the rage and fear building in her mind. She needed to focus. The beast could be loosed on Hunter, but not yet, not until Evee and Anna were safe.

Susan found herself moving toward the source of the blood. Her feet hushed by the snow, she stalked silent as a shadow toward it. Around a tree stump, Susan caught a patch of silver fur glinting in the starlight, then another. It was strange, the patches were close together, but didn't form a discernible shape. Then Susan put the pieces together and saw Evee's outline, patches of silver fur connected by dark matted ones streaked with blood. Susan recoiled from the sight. Evee's hands were pinned to the tree with silver spikes, her head bowed forward against her chest and her breathing ragged.

Susan crept along, right up behind Evee's tree, leaning out to free a hand from one of the silver spikes. Evee's eyes cracked open and she looked up at Susan, pleading, "No... run..."

Susan could feel the cold metal of the spike beneath her palm, but before she could tear it out, a stabbing pain in her side made her drop to the ground. She screamed as the pain radiated through her veins like fire. A shadow lurched past her, wrenching something from her side and the pain receded. Anna and Evee cried out before she hit the snow. Susan fell to her knees, collapsing at Hunter's feet.

Hunter leaned over Susan, holding up a thin metal pin blackened with her blood. He ran his tongue along it, savouring the taste. "Oh Sue, you shouldn't have come, but now I get two for the price of one."

"Run!" Susan yelled at Anna, while lunging toward Hunter. She caught his ankle in her jaws and felt her teeth sink into flesh. A blow to the face stunned her and a scream opened her mouth as pain pierced her shoulder. Hunter flung her back against the ground and pushed the spike further, jamming it into the ground. Susan kicked him in the gut, pushing him off and reached to pull the spike out, but she was too slow. Another spike pierced her opposite hand, pinning her fully to the ground. Susan thrashed against the pins, but the pain was overwhelming. All she could do was cry and struggle to breathe as the fire of the pins burned through her body.

"I love silver," Hunter stood over her gloating.

"Let them go!" Anna screamed.

Susan swore. Anna should have run while she had the chance. Now all three of them would die here.

"I don't know," Hunter mused, "Two for one, hardly seems fair."

"But I'm the one you want aren't I?"

"Who says I don't want these two as well?"

"I've already escaped once. Can you handle losing me again?"

Hunter lifted a foot, hovering over the pin in Susan's hand. He stepped down and Susan couldn't hold back her scream. The world swam in and out of her vision and she begged, "Run dammit! Run!"

"No, I don't think Anna's going anywhere and neither are you! How about I kill you while she watches?"

Hunter crouched over Susan, who froze. Every time she struggled against the pins pain ripped through her, but if she didn't try to move, Hunter would kill her. Susan wondered if this was how Jim felt in his last moments. Terrified, in pain and betrayed by someone he thought he could trust. Maybe this was justice. If only Anna and Evee could get away.

Hunter lurched to the side as Anna crashed into him with such ferocity they went spinning head over heels together into a gully. Susan strained to see, but they had fallen out of her range of vision. Nausea filled Susan and she knew Anna had lost the fight. The struggling subsided and Hunter emerged from the trees, tossing Anna down beside where Susan lay.

"Get off her! Don't touch her!" A new wave of rage washed over Susan.

Hunter pounced on Anna's back pinning her hands to the ground. Disgust fuelled Susan's rage. He was playing with them like toys. "You're a sick bastard, you know that!"

"You have no idea," Hunter grinned wickedly as the low light reflected in his eyes like an animal's. "I'm sorry Sue, it's been fun, but I think it's time to finish the game."

"No!" Susan howled, tearing her flesh against the pins, but they burned and sapped her strength, forcing her to stay down. She tilted her head back looking up at the stars, her vision blurring with tears. "Oh God, I'm sorry. Anna, Jim, I'm so sorry. Nobody should die like this."

In that moment, everything went still and Susan felt Evee and Anna beside her. They were both terrified, screaming in fear and pain. She could hear them calling, feel the waves of panic emanating from them, but somehow, Susan felt detached. These expressions of fear and pain weren't them. For the first time, she had a clear sense of their essence, only because Hunter was about to destroy it.

Susan's inner beast stirred, but it was unlike anything she had felt before. Fear and anger brought out a raging beast, from inside her, but what was trying to surface now was completely different. Warmth spread from her heart, flowing through her veins, fighting against the searing pain from the pins. She might still be a slave to the beast, but it was stronger than fear or anger. The beast could run on other emotions like the love welling in her heart. Hope bloomed, and Susan felt its cooling presence in her blood.

Hunter's mouth dipped toward Anna's neck. Anna's eyes widened in fear, but Susan reached out to her with all the love and hope in her heart. It didn't matter that she couldn't physically move. She and Anna were connected by something deeper. Susan opened the bond between them, calling out to Anna's heart driving back the fear permeating their world with all the love she could muster. Susan lay bare her love for her friends, her family, her pack, and for life itself. In that moment she was surrounded by peace despite the chaos around her. She reached out with her bond and shared it with Anna and Evee.

Hope glinted in Anna's eyes and an understanding passed between them. Even with Hunter's fangs grazing her neck, Anna became calm. She surrendered to Susan's projected feelings. Then Anna's body twitched violently. Muscles snapped and bones creaked as her features contorted. Susan could feel Anna's pain and bewilderment, but she knew what it meant. Anna was shifting.

Hunter crouched above Anna laughing at what he must have thought was her struggling. Before he could realize what was happening, a wolf sat under him. Anna lunged at his face. The two locked together, in a deadly fight.

Strength surged through Susan's body. She wasn't going to watch anyone else she loved die. She tore her hand all the way through the silver pin, cringing at the pain. But now the burning of the silver was gone and she felt even stronger. Reaching for her shoulder she ripped out the other pin and sprang to her feet.

Leaping into the fray, Susan grabbed Hunter's shoulder and pulled him back from Anna, exposing his throat. Anna leapt forward, teeth met flesh and a scream died on Hunter's lips, turning to spluttering and gurgling as life was choked out of him. His body went limp beneath Susan and she released her hold, backing away. She tripped and fell, too exhausted to steady herself. The ground was cold against her bare skin. Susan looked at her hands, realizing she was human again. The beast had released her.

Susan stared at the scene before her. The dark wolf that was Anna finally released Hunter's neck from her jaws. They both watched the mangled body, afraid it might spring to life once more, but it remained still. Just like that, Hunter was dead. He couldn't hurt them anymore.

Anna leaned her head back and let out a howl. Susan didn't take her eyes from the corpse until a cold nose poked her leg. She ran her hands through Anna's fur, making sure she was real. Her black fur seemed to absorb all the light around them and amber eyes sparkled back at Susan. She pulled Anna into a big hug and went to bury her face in the wolf's fur, but Anna pulled away and trotted over to the tree stump.

"Evee!" Susan sprang to her feet, almost falling over, but found her balance and shifted into a werewolf at the same time, covering her body in warm fur again. Susan managed to scramble over to where Evee was pinned. Susan yanked out the silver pins. Evee flinched with every withdrawal but then her muscles relaxed and relief flooded her face. With the last pin out, she slumped forward, holding her wounded hands close to her body.

Anna, nuzzled gently at Evee's arms and began to lick the wounds. Evee stared at her in awe, then at Susan. "I can't believe it. How did you do it?" She pushed Anna back, catching her breath as her brows knit together, "And how could you both be so stupid! You could have been killed!"

"We could say the same to you! How could you go off like that without telling anyone? Without taking all of us with you? We're a family now, you can't escape us Evee!"

Anna grumbled something unintelligible in agreement.

Evee laughed, her voice ringing through the trees in sheer relief. "Like mother, like pups I guess." Evee tried to get to her feet but faltered and slumped back down into the snow. Susan went to hold her up, wrapping her arms around Evee's shoulders. Anna pushed up against her side as well and the three of them sat holding each other until howling began in the distance.

"Sure, now they come, after the danger's over!" Evee winced, extracting herself from the girls to sit upright on her own.

"Do you think we'll be in trouble?" Susan laughed.

"When are you two not in trouble?" Evee grumbled. "Not that it matters, we have each other, so everything will be alright."

"I hope so..." Susan let the thought trail off through her spinning head. She couldn't shake the feeling that danger was still present, even though Hunter was dead. Her mind kept drifting back to that moment between life and death when she was able to open her heart. She wasn't sure what she had stumbled upon, but she knew it was the most powerful and moving thing she had ever known. Her ever changing world stood still in the dark, waiting for that power to find its way through her again.

Sabine Wilder is a writer and artist from Sudbury Ontario. *Runaway* is her debut novel and Sabine would love to hear feedback from readers about her book. Discover more about Sabine and her work at sabinewilder.com.

Made in the USA
Columbia, SC
13 June 2021

40089888R00111